Ben Peek's *Twenty-Six Lies/One Truth* is inebriating, an absinthe of self-deception, a smoke-filled room of conflicted emotion, a hall of mirrors, each of them distorting both perception and reality. Ben Peek dances on the stepping stones of Ben Peek's supposed life, leaping from philosophy to pop culture, from insight to angst. As one reads this remarkable work, the question arises, "what is the line between the art and the artist"? Peek knows. I know. But you cannot know, for certain, until you pick out the lies. Do you trust your judgment that much? Do you trust Ben Peek? What makes you so certain that you can crack the code of *Twenty-Six Lies/One Truth*? I'd be careful if I were you. Deception awaits.

Forrest Aguirre
World Fantasy Award-winning editor of Leviathan 3 and 4

Twenty-Six Lies/ One Truth

Ben Peek

Twenty-Six Lies/ One Truth

the autobiography of a man who
has been nowhere, done nothing
and met nobody

by

Ben Peek

Wheatland Press
http://www.wheatlandpress.com

Twenty-Six Lies/One Truth

Published by

Wheatland Press

http://www.wheatlandpress.com
P. O. Box 1818
Wilsonville, OR 97070

Library of Congress Cataloging-in-Publication data is available upon request.
ISBN 0-9755903-8-3
Printed in the United States of America
Interior by Deborah Layne.
Original cover art by Andrew Macrae.
Original illustrations by Anna Brown.

A

Abortion, Event – We are twenty-four and have been broken up for three weeks when I drive us to the clinic. I am flat broke and the driver's window of my '74 Mazda had been smashed, the radio stolen; but I pay the two hundred and forty dollars for the procedure and tell R that money isn't a problem. I want do something. I want to show that I am part of it, that it is as much me as it is her, and so I do the monetary side, the driving side, and R does her part with doctors and nurses standing around her in a sterile white room. Afterward, R lies in the back of the car and, lost in the post-procedural haze of anesthesia, whispers, over and over, "There is no baby, no baby, no baby."

Autobiography – How much can you trust authors who write their own history?

Apartment, A Dialogue –

Hey.

I hate your cock!

...

Well, there's a hello for me.

I guess you've been throwing up?

You see the bucket?

Yes, I do.

I've been sick.

It's a lovely bucket. I especially like the Hello Kitty stickers.

I wanted pictures of wrestlers but they were out.

You can't win all the time. It is cute when you pout and whimper, though.

It's not fair. I want to puke in a bucket of wrestlers.

...

How was your day?

Not as exciting as yours. Is this glass clean?

Yes.

Are your students boring?

The ones who don't talk are, yeah; but most are okay. Some of them are starting to push themselves. I saw a piece of concrete poetry that was pretty neat. It was shaped in George W. Bush's head, but the words were taken from speeches he had given on terrorism. Was pretty cool.

Sounds difficult to read.

It was more of a visual thing. So...stay home tonight?

No—

—Ow!

I sat up too quick.

You okay?

I've been waiting all week for this. You're not canceling now.

You can't take your bucket, you know?

Don't be a cunt.

Albert, Laura – Albert is the author responsible for the J.T. LeRoy persona. Born in 1965 and raised in Brooklyn, she spent her time as an actor, phone sex operator, and a guitarist in the band Daddy Don't Go, before entering the public light as LeRoy in 2001. In her first novel, *Sarah*, she presented an author who was, in no particular order, a teenage, HIV positive, transgendered, homeless drug addict who had worked as a lot lizard—a male prostitute in truck stops— and who was now writing a thinly disguised memoir of his/her life. Part of the success of *Sarah* was that LeRoy's own life lent a reality to the books that allowed the audience to feel as if they were getting a truth that they, for the most part, would never be associated with. After the revelation that LeRoy was fiction, Albert was attacked about her credibility to present such experiences without being seen to exploit them. Since Albert had not "survived" LeRoy's life, she was now seen as a day tripper, a white woman cashing in on the freak level that allowed for such a life to be automatically dramatic, and she was now accused of misrepresenting and taking advantage of all the teenage, HIV positive, transgendered, homeless drug addicts who worked as lot lizards in the world. Unlike those who bought the books, of course.

A Silver Mt Zion - A Silver Mt. Zion are a band that is now called Thee Silver Mt. Zion Orchestra & Tra-La-La Band. They change their name on every album. For their first album, *He Has Left Us Alone But Shafts of Light Sometimes Grace the Corner of Our Rooms*, they were simply a Silver Mt. Zion; for the second, *Born Into Trouble as the Sparks Fly Upwards*, they were the Silver Mt. Zion Orchestra & Tra-La-La Band; for the third *"This is Our Punk-Rock," Thee Rusted Satellites Gather and Sing*, the Silver Mt. Zion Memorial Orchestra & Tra-La-La Band with Choir; for the ep *Pretty Little Lightening Paw*, they were Thee Silver Mountain Reveries; and for their latest album, *Horses in the Sky*, Thee Silver Mt. Zion Orchestra & Tra-La-La Band. Do you think it frustrates them, then, that people don't use the new band name for each album? Or is it simply that changing your band name, no matter how subtly, from album to album, is simply too pretentious even for anyone to take seriously.

Amnesiac - I am fascinated with amnesia. I daydream about what it would be like to have amnesia and to wake up with a clean slate. To have lost my past, my friends, my jobs, my bank accounts, my degrees, my publications, my albums, and my books. To have lost everything. Would I fight to get it back? Would I become someone different? Would my environment alter me? The memories of my friends? Would I like the person I was told about?

Australia – I am Australian.

Art? A Dialogue —

> Hold my bucket while I get dressed.

It smells.

> Your cock did that.

My cock has never smelt like this.

> You've never been that close.

It's all that vertebrae.

...

Hey, I did get a cool email today.

Yeah?

Yeah.
A publisher in the States wants to do a book with me. A small book—about forty-thousand words.

Hey!

That is *super* cool!

Aw, look at that, I get hugs.

You're pretty proud of yourself, aren't you?

Yeah.

Good.

(Sit down. You've been on your feet all day.)

(It was just the afternoon.)

(Don't argue.)

Did you know the publisher before this?

Not much. She bought a short story from me a month ago.

Why the offer then?

7

She reads my blog, and I've been doing these entries about letters on it—sort of creating an autobiography out of them. People have dug them. She *really* digs them. She reckons they'd make a neat book, so...you know.

This is *so* cool.

It is, isn't it? Like I'm Audrey Hepburn in a fucking diner.

I thought she was in a cafe.

Either way.

Is this one paying well?

Pays a bit, but not much. It's—

An *art* thing.

Yeah.

You gotta start making proper money from this soon.

Don't start on that.

I'm just saying.

Come on, not tonight. Just be happy for me tonight.

Autobiography – There are ghostwriters for those in the world who are famous, but illiterate. At times, I imagine unhappy, sad, greying men and women in front of computers struggling to get by from cheque to cheque, forcing themselves to imagine what it would be like to be shiny and glamorous so that an audience of struggling men and women can purchase the book about their shiny and glamorous "life".

Abortion, Thought – R and I aborted our child. It was, however, the word child that lingered in me. Of the abortion itself, I could not have been better with it. Neither of us believed that sperm and ovary meant life had begun and that life must be cherished. We knew where we were in our lives, and what we could, and could not, be responsible for. But the word child is not empty. It is filled with expectations and meaning and, since I am a guy who spends his time with words and how they can be used best, the word lingered, sticky with concepts; with the idea that a tiny, new life would be dependent on me; that I would be partly responsible for it. The word child, I found, did not need a tangible counter part to dig into your mind in the quiet moments before sleep. It existed, there, in my imagination without the need for air and food, fed by an umbilical cord of language. There was no way to remove it.

B

Blog. Personal Diary Entry, March 3rd – *Tonight: dinner, a celebration. I have agreed to write a book based off entries on my blog. I have signed a contract. The publisher wants a book written in alphabetic chapters. Twenty six chapters, beginning with A, ending with Z, and with ten entries in each chapter. Two hundred and sixty entries, all up. I was just playing around before. Performing in public. Now, with a publisher, I can push the idea further, turn it into a self contained thing. I emailed the publisher and asked about my boundaries. She told me I had none. I told her I what I planned, and she said, 'Don't be afraid. Go further.'*

Ben Peek – I was born Benjamin Michael Peek, but it is a name I never use. On one rental card for a video store in Seven Hills—where I never rent anything—I am Dr. Benjamin Peek; but for everything else, I am just Ben, and Ben Peek when I am required to sign something. I was once told that I look like the kind of guy whose name is two syllables long.

Brando, Marlon (Surrogate Father Figure #1) – I grew up in a city with five television channels: the ABC, Seven, Nine, Ten, and SBS. On channel Ten in the 80s there was a midday movie every weekday: old black and white movies, for the most part, and each of

11

them filled with grey coloured Americans such as Humphrey Bogart, Joseph Cotten, and Janet Leigh. The films were introduced by a large, effeminate sounding man named Bill Collins. One day when I was home sick from school, Collins introduced On the Waterfront, and it was there that I first saw Marlon Brando. It struck me that here was a man who had given himself over to desires and who was violent, vulnerable, but always charismatic. Afterward, I hunted down old Brando films in the local video store. Mum didn't understand, but she hated Brando, and said so; I told her that in his films he was passionate, and not afraid to be anyone.

Beasts of Bourbon, the – In 2005, the Beasts of Bourbon reunite and begin touring. One night in Brisbane, I try to sneak into one of their gigs, pretending to be a roadie. It is not one of my better ideas.

Ben Peek, Date of Birth – 12th October, 1976.

Ben Peek, Image –

Ben Peek, Place of Birth – I was born in Blacktown Hospital at quarter to eight in the evening, after twenty-one hours of labour.

Boyfriend First, Girlfriend Second: Introducing Geraldine Lee –

Butler, Octavia – The first novel of Octavia Butler's that I read was *Parable of the Sower*. O bought it for me because I had not read much science fiction. I had grown up with TV sci fi and, even now, I prefer the image driven versions of the genre to the prose ones. I like the spectacle. When I explained this, she told me that I hadn't found the right science fiction and in that, she was right: Butler was different. But then Butler was different to most writers, no matter the genre. On a craft level, her prose was deceptively simple, her sentence structure plain and unadorned. Emotions, descriptions, and ideas were laid out carefully, methodically in her paragraphs, with each layered on top of the other. What made it work, however, was Butler's passion for all humans, for the questions of race, gender, and sexuality; for the way in which we, as people, live. Butler was acutely aware that there was no such thing as black and white when it came

13

to morality, and the fiction she wrote was grey, complex, beautiful, and kind. I respected her as I did few authors who lived (it is a hard thing to respect the living unconditionally). When she died, in 2006, outside her home in Seattle, the sadness I felt was almost unseemly, given that I had never met her. I would never have met her, given a chance, since I believe it best if you do not meet the authors you admire. You hope, however, that they do not die at the age of fifty-eight.

Books – I wrote my first novel when I was twenty-three. Old authors tell new authors that they will never sell their first novel, but that's usually because the old authors did not sell theirs, and have failed to realise that the market has grown. It took me five years to sell mine. Titled *Black Sheep* it was a dystopian novel set in an alternate Sydney, where anyone who was not Australian in thought was sentenced to be Assimilated, a new punishment that stripped out the skin colour, identity, and memory from the individual. After the punishment, they were referred to by numbers and given basic government jobs like driving taxis. Agents told me it was too niche market, though they never explained what that meant, and so I took it to mean that they couldn't make money off it. After agents, the publishers who I could get to read it told me it that it was too dark, too intense, and too relentless. I thought that would be a good thing, but apparently not. After I went through all the independent publishers in Australia, an independent publisher in America liked it and bought it. By this time, I was two years into writing my second novel, a mosaic exploration of present day Sydney. I still remember when the email came. I was, firstly, surprised. I sat there for at least a minute without thought. Pleasure came after. Then I wondered who I could tell.

C

Cunt – As a word, cunt is considered, amongst many, to be the nastiest word in the English language. I have friends who won't say it. They say, 'I won't say *it*,' or, 'No, I don't like the C-word.' Each one of these friends of mine are female. Now, I am not in the habit of telling my friends how they should or should not think, but it has always struck me as deeply, deeply wrong that cunt is considered by women to be the foulest word in the English language.

Cunt – The history of cunt from Wikipedia: "Cunt is an old Germanic word, and appeared as cunte in Middle English and kunta in Old Norse. It has cognates in most Germanic languages, such as the Swedish and Old Norwegian kunta, Frisian kunte, and Dutch kut (while kont in Dutch means bum, strangely the Dutch word for 'cunt', the earlier mentioned 'kut', is considered to be considerably less offensive in the Dutch speaking areas than cunt is in the English speaking world). Interestingly, the Afrikaans word 'kont' is equivalent to the English 'cunt' and is even more offensive to Afrikaans-speakers than 'cunt' is for English-speakers. It goes back to an Old Germanic stem kunton." Boring, isn't it?

Cunt – Rumour has it that Australians are fascinated with the word. Certainly I am, at the very least. It is said, however, that if the Australian male (perhaps bronzed, blond and able to surf) wants to make a misogynistic comment towards a woman that he is less likely than any other male in the English speaking world to use cunt in a derogatory way. That is because, to the Australian male (white, sun browned, living in the bush) the word cunt is used in a friendly, joking way. Instead, the Australian male (these images are incorrectly white) shows his fascination in the creation of synonyms for cunt. Ugly, nasty words like slag, slapper, bushpig, and slurry. Just let that last one roll off your tongue slowly, the tongue pressed hard against the top of your mouth as you say it. *Slurry*. That's one nasty word.

Cunt – Some of the other synonyms for cunt from around the world are golden axe-wound, ham-wallet, oyster-ditch, fuckhole, tuna taco, gutted ewok and yellow-bearded clam.

Cunt – I have taught (and still do teach) creative writing at a number of places. In one of the programs, I have students write an angry letter. The idea is to get them to consider how they use their sentences and how it can be altered for emotion. Short is very popular for anger. You yell. You. Show. Your. *Hate*. Spit words. Spit sentences. Swear. CUNT! I once shouted at a class, while standing on a table. DON'T YOU WANT TO SHOW SOMEONE YOU HATE THEM! CALL THEM A CUNT! A FUCKING CUNT! Twenty minutes later I convinced them to write a love letter, referencing cunts (their own or the cunt of their loved one, even if they didn't like cunts, sexually speaking).

Cunt – For a while, I thought about writing erotica. Y, an American author of erotica, told me that the word cunt was rarely used. In pornography it had its place, but as a word for erotica, cunt was not considered to be very erotic. Pussy was very popular, apparently, and so was slit, sex, opening and, though it sounds ridiculous, coochie.

Cunt · It *is* deeply insulting that the word cunt can be considered the foulest word in the English language. This is a fight often fought by feminists and I cannot show them enough admiration for taking up this battle. There are words such as corporate, clinic, and corduroy, all of which start with the letter c, and all of which deserve to be put on the list of offending words in English. But mostly, it's the fact that the foulest word in the English language refers to the female genitals that offends me. I have always thought very kindly about female genitals, personally. I wonder how men would feel if someone told them that cock had just become the most insulting word in the English language? If someone was to tell me that my cock was considered the physical manifestation of the foulest word in the English language, I'd be pretty fucking pissed off.

Cunt – X, who is gay, once had a job pretending to be a woman on an online sex chat channel. He referred to his cunt as a meat curtain.

Cunt – One of the most depressing things I have ever encountered in relation to the word cunt was when I was teaching a year three class. One of the boys in the class had the word cunt written on his homework. I asked him about it, and he told me that his brother wrote it, and that he didn't know what it meant. By the time he had finished, the rest of the class wanted to know what the word was, so he told them. Most of them didn't know what it meant. They screamed it out, testing the word, and said it in a variety of ways. Mostly loudly. I wondered what the teacher in the class next door thought, then decided I didn't care. Only one student in my class knew what it meant; *she* refused to say it, telling everyone that it was the *baddest* word, and that her Mum and Dad said she wasn't to use it. Ever. After hearing that I decided to test all the parents, so I told all the kids to go home and ask their parents what cunt meant. I spelt the word for them when I was asked, and watched as they wrote the word CUNT neatly on the back of their hands and in the margin of their homework. The following week, when they came back, they each told me that they had asked their parents, and that they had been told that it was the baddest and rudest word and that they weren't to say it. *Ever.* Like I said, it just about the most depressing thing.

Cunt – Cunt was once a term of endearment between myself and someone important to me.

17

D

Depression – I suffer from clinical depression. At least, this is what I am told, and if you can't believe the psychiatrist you've seen for the last six years, who can you believe? My Bombay-born psychiatrist works in the public health care system, which means that he bulk bills, and that people without a decent income can see him. It is how I see him. However, this means that he is chronically overworked, that there are always new patients arriving, and that there are not enough leaving. If I am lucky, I will see him for more than fifteen minutes, before he gives me the yellow and white script for my pills.

Demidenko, Helen – In 1993, Helen Demidenko won the Vogel Literary Award for her novel *The Hand that Signed the Paper*. The Vogel is an annual award given to the "best" unpublished first novel by an Australian under the age of thirty-five in that year. Authors such as Tim Winton and Mandy Sayer have gotten their start in the award. What set Demidenko apart from authors who had won it before, however, was her Ukrainian heritage, and the way that she used it to lay the foundation for her novel. Reportedly, *The Hand that Signed the Paper* told the story of a pair of brothers in a Ukrainian family who, having survived Stalinism, became members of a Nazi death squad before, finally, Australian citizens. I use the word reportedly here because the book fell out of print after the Ukrainian Demidenko, who appeared in public as a tall, blonde European woman in traditional Ukrainian dresses and who spoke with the odd

Ukrainian word peppered throughout her speech, was revealed to be Helen Darville, and Darville was not Ukrainian at all. When this was revealed, Demidenko/Darville had already won the prestigious Miles Franklin Prize and been awarded the Australian Literature Society Gold Medal. The media attacks focused upon the fact that the validity of her fiction relied on her heritage, which, now that it had been revealed to be false, suddenly cast her book in an anti-Semitic light, and had many calling Darville racist. What the media did not focus on, however, was the suggestion that Darville had plagiarised much of the book from Graham Greene's *The Power and the Glory* and Elizabeth Bowen's *the Demon Lover.*

Dancing – L convinces me to go dancing two months after my return to Sydney. Her boyfriend refuses to go, but I have no objection. Maybe it will even be fun. Besides which, dancing has always looked sexy on TV; I am curious to see if I will be able to move like *that.* The classes are at six thirty, Monday nights. Two hours. I learn to Cha-Cha-Cha, Salsa, and Swing. The instructor is a tiny, fat, hugely pot bellied man, but he can move like *that.* I, however, am obviously a cripple.

Dysfunctional – I don't make a big deal out of being depressed. It is not the first thing that I tell someone when I meet them, but it is not the last, either. It is simply a thing, neither good nor bad, and I take the pills and I go through my life. This is because I *can* go through life. I've never been institutionalised. I've never had over two hundred dollars worth of medication. I've never been unable to afford my medication. I've never been completely unable to get out of bed. I have never parked my car in the garage, taken the green garden hose and run it from the exhaust pipe and into the driver's side window, and then turned the car on. I have never been fucked up in the hundreds of ways that you can be fucked up with depression. On the scale of things, I'm lucky. A handful of friends (and sometimes people who are not friends) that I have known over the years have not been as lucky as me. So I don't make a big deal out of it. Instead, I just try and keep myself good, and I do this by self management. The key, I've found, is a mix of pills, activity, and keeping my mind off things in that slightly obsessive way I have. Whenever I feel myself slipping, I rustle up a bit of work, either paid or volunteer. Some days are better than others, but that's the nature of it.

Death, the Belief – I was cured, at a very young age, of a curiosity towards death. To me, the act of dying—death, as I see it—is about pain. Be it quick or slow, dying is about the connection between our mortal body and less mortal soul being sawn through by a jagged, rusty knife. My opinion can be shrunk down to two words: Dying Sucks. And though I am confident about the idea that a part of me will exist afterwards, I'm not that confident that it will be a conscious part of me. The *after*life attempts, by its nature, to render death as an event that is part of a larger journey, and it tries to assure you that life will go on, and that you needn't be afraid. On the surface, it sounds all good, but the truth is, it depends on what kind of belief you have. Maybe you're just sitting around waiting for Jesus to come back. Maybe you're reincarnated as a God or a worm. Maybe you get a paradise. Maybe you don't. Maybe you are just on the stopover between destinations, but then again, maybe not. I fail to see how anyone can be certain of any choice, but then, I suppose, that is the point of faith.

Death, the Experience After – After a person has died, it's all about the living. I had never really thought about this until I was reading the undertaker poet turned essayist, Thomas Lynch, and his collection of essays, *The Undertaking*. The dead don't care, he writes, only the living care. Only the living care about how the dead are buried. About how the body looks in the casket. About a casket, in fact. Only the living worry if the body has a nice suit or dress on. Only the living worry if the body is lifelike. Though Lynch never follows it, the logic of this continues into the rituals that, as a society, we have for (and concerning) the afterlife. They too are for the living. It is the living who talk about the dead being happy, being out of pain, about being near them. Living TV evangelists and spiritualists can even see the dead standing next to the living, trapped in some hateful, half life where their only desire is to tell the living it is fine, go on without me. And if they are not waiting there, they are in Heaven (or Hell), waiting for the living. It is not confined to Western beliefs, either. On the Day of the Dead, the spirits of children return on November 1st, and adults on the 2nd. The dead are haunting us in a variety of forms, but not because they want it, but because we do. We demand that they exist in a way that we can understand. We demand that they haunt us through our rituals and the memories we keep.

Departure, A Dialogue –

Ready?

...

Hello?

B!

...Yeah?

I'm ready.

Sorry. Thinking about the book.

Let's go.

Delight – In Western culture, the confessional narrative allows for us to admit to our pain, our suffering, and hopefully, our redemption. We are encouraged to do this, even. TV shows have become confessional temples where "real" people own up to cheating, lying and then finding God. They are quite popular because we, the audience, sit in the elevated, voyeuristic position of judgment over the individual, no matter our own personal experiences. But the confessional narrative resists pleasure, unless it is at the end of pain, and is functioning as a reward, or if it is a non-selfish, socially supported function. I love my children, for example, is something that we in the audience can understand and accept. If, however, we hear, 'I love the feel or the juice from an orange running down my chin,' or 'I love anal sex', then we respond differently. We consider leaving, and if we stay, we do so, uncomfortable. Later, amongst friends, we might ridicule it.

Darville, Helen – Once known as Helen Demidenko, Helen Darville, having been forced to return to her old name, continued to write for newspapers around the country, though she was primarily based in Queensland. In 1997, she was again accused of plagiarism, this time for a column about being an Evil Overlord, which she reportedly copy and pasted from an email and claimed was her own. After being fired, she continued to write articles for various papers, and was accused again of being anti-Semite after an interview with infamous Holocaust denier, David Irving, in 2000. Darville herself never agreed with him publicly, but that point seems to make little difference. Two years later, she began studying a law degree in Queensland, and is now working as an Associate to the Supreme Court under the name Helen Dale. To help finance her law degree, she auctioned off the Australian Literature Society's gold medal, which, even though Darville is contemptible as an author, does contain a certain amount of admiration as a fuck you gesture to Australian literature.

Depression – How I ended up in the tiny office of a Bombay born psychiatrist is not due to any single event but, rather, a culmination of events from the past and (at the time) present. It was mostly caused by a growing dissatisfaction with my life and my inability to change it. It is not a very dramatic story, I'm afraid. What came after is of much more interest. Here, I am talking about the drug induced rebirth. For the first time in my life I was capable of reaching through that incapacitating haze that had surrounded my life to make conscious choices. It is a strange thing to realise that you have lived for such a time that you can not remember making decisions and that you have, instead, drifted along, dealing with what life, people, and everything else put in front of you, full well knowing that none of it really interested you. It is stranger, however, to suddenly realise this is no longer the case.

E

Eliot, George – Born in 1819, dead by 1880, Mary Anne Evans, Marian, to her friends, was the English author George Eliot. She adopted the pseudonym of a man, she said, so that her work would be taken seriously.

Earth (The Indian Place Run by Hippies) –

Ekistics, Geography – I grew up in a suburb called Toongabbie. It is located in what is now known as the middle of the Western Suburbs of Sydney, though in 1976, when I was born there, it was what many considered the edge. Only scrub and bushland lay beyond it. These days, the streets, factories, and houses in Toongabbie spread across the land like a stain across a series of low hills, before connecting to Pendle Hill, Winston Hills, and Seven Hills, its neighbouring suburbs. Toongabbie itself is cut in half by two train lines with one narrow bridge crossing it. On the Western side, there is a low, ugly shopping centre, old apartment blocks without security doors, a housing commission, and burnt out cars that appear once a month on the side of the road. They remain there for a week or two before the council pulls them away. The Eastern side of the suburb is defined by a long, twisting trench of concrete creek that plows through the ground. Every winter as a kid, it flooded, leaving my mother with a fear of floods. Around the creek are low, flat houses made from brick and weatherboard and fibro, each hidden behind fences of wood and colourbond that have been covered in graffiti. Three or four blocks back from the houses on the South are factories, while in the North are the public schools. These days, the whole suburb sits at the end of the M4 and on the side of James Ruse Drive, which are both freeways strung with cars every morning and evening. You have to pay a toll on the M4, however. Historically, Toongabbie is the Third Settlement, meaning that it was the third piece of land that the British stole from the Aboriginal people after they invaded, but no one much cares about that in the area. It's just a nothing bit of Sydney on the side of roads that go somewhere.

Ethics – When T was thirteen, I was her tutor for literature. She was in the second year of High School and wanted someone to listen to her. Someone who wasn't thirteen, who wasn't her family, and who wasn't going to judge her. I guess I looked like a pretty good choice, and I suppose I was, because I listened. She had good taste in music, so-so taste in books, hated her home life, and was bisexual. One day, I mentioned it to J, showing him how my job did some good, but his immediate response was that *I* should be careful. I didn't want to end up in a situation that would get *me* into trouble, apparently. It had never occurred to me that I could be in danger, just for listening to a thirteen year old girl. If I had been female, I wondered, would the danger have been lessened? Apparently. Out of curiousity, I ran the story by a couple of my other friends, and each responded in the same way. In the end, I ignored each of them, and continued doing what I had. I still do it. It is the easiest thing in the world.

Experience – If cloning was legal, I would clone myself, ten, maybe fifteen times, and then put the baby Ben's in different environments around the world. I would do this to monitor just how different "I" was after having grown up in radically different environments.

Ekistics, Economics – Toongabbie is a working class suburb. The majority of people living in it work in the factories in the area, or in service jobs, such as selling fried chicken out of Jenny's Choice Chicken, or in supermarkets and such. None of the wages are great, and a good portion of people in the area pick up child support, especially if they're a one income family. When their kids are old enough, they pick up the government study allowance, Austudy. The average income where both parents work allows for them to pay the mortgage, buy the groceries, keep your car running, and save a little. Maybe you get a night out, if you're lucky. That was how it was in the house I grew up in, though we never worried about rent, since my father's life insurance paid off the house for the family. Essentially, my father's death meant that his family never had to worry about rent, but it also meant that we were chained to Toongabbie. Things weren't all that easy, however, and because of a widow's pension, Mum's job was taxed as a second income. For years, the grocery bill was just added to the always existing credit card bill. We ate in debt, even as we ate in the world of cheap generic brands. However, for all that, I had friends who lived in apartments where the roof was falling down, and who divided the living room of their house into extra bedrooms. I was always conscious of how lucky we were.

Equality – We are not born equal. A boy born in Toongabbie has more opportunities than a girl born in a poor village in Ethiopia. To have equality, you must work for it.

Ethnicity – My wallpaper is the image of two Israeli girls, both eleven, maybe twelve, sitting in front of a row of explosives. The bombs are going to be dropped on Lebanon and one of the girls has written, "From Israel and Danielle." I keep it, not because it illustrates how a new generation will grow up with the same prejudices, but because I imagine the photographers, the parents, and the soldiers, all of them standing around, watching the two girls draw. Standing around and not once thinking that they should stop them. Instead, they take photos. They take photos of happy, innocent girls drawing on bombs, and then sell them to the media outlets around the world. They don't see a problem with this.

Ekistics, Sociology – Toongabbie is straight, nuclear family, Christian value suburb. Most of the people in the area are one form of Christianity or another, and when they are not, the values that they keep are still that of the straight, nuclear family. No doubt there are people in the area who do not subscribe to this, but as a majority, this is true. As a majority, we grow up being told to work hard, respect our elders, study, and when you leave school, you should get a job. As a whole, people in Toongabbie believe that voting is important, that you shouldn't steal, that sport is good, and that you should get married, buy a house, and work until retirement, at which case you ought to have saved a bit. But for all that this sounds like a very white, Western point of view, Toongabbie has always had a strong Asian community, and nearly half the people in the street that I grew up in were Asian, at one time or another. They were from the Philippines, for the most part, though some came from Vietnam, and still more came from Egypt and India.

Echo – I am eleven and the school has taken us on an excursion to the Jenolan Caves. The Caves are in the Blue Mountains, about two hours by bus, give or take, and we sit in it and talk loudly for the entire trip, any crash responsibility signed away by permission slips. As a collection of skin colour and heritage and language, we are white Australian, Samoan, Lebanese, Sri Lankan, Turkish, Vietnamese, Maltese, and Greek, amongst others. At the Caves, we are put into class groups, and we follow a guide through the dark, twisting caves. We are given sheets to fill in. We are told to stay away from the edges. Everything is coloured different and I cannot resist looking over. Half way through, our guide, a tall Aboriginal man, stops, and tells us to scream into the dark so that we can hear our echoes come back. We do. All thirty of us do. We scream at the same time. Our voices carry away from us, down into the dark, and return, garbled, mixed, a mongrel breed of vocals, a thing without clear or concise origin. It is a new thing. A thing born from our throats. A thing for the future.

most of his life in the city until his death in 1994. *Factotum*, his second novel, while being very similar to his first, *Post Office*, has the distinction of being an actually well written book, and is the one I recommend over the other. Both books, however, are centred around a man called Henry Chinaski, an alcoholic womaniser who drifts from job to bar to woman in an attempt to avoid the mind numbing regularity of his life and jobs (for Chinaski is, as the title suggests, a man who does many different kinds of work, though he has little love for any of it). As Bukowski himself noted, Chinaski was really a thinly described autobiographical character for himself, and much of what happened in the books and short fiction that featured Chinaski were drawn from the author's own life. Even, I believe, the rape scene in *Post Office*.

Funeral – At my first funeral, I get to sit up front. It is in a big Catholic church, with the stained glass windows colouring the air around me in specs of drifting, bright, multicoloured light. The pews are hard, however. When I look back into the crowd, I see the neighbours. My uncles and aunts are around us. Even my Mum's sister, who lives in Darwin. All four of my grandparents are there. It is the only time they are all together in my memory. Of the service itself, I remember only the priest, talking about how proud my father was of my sister, but never once mentioning me. I pay strict attention, but I am never mentioned. When I ask my mother about this lapse, she quietly, but firmly, hushes me.

Factotum – Bukowski was an asshole. There is no if, maybe, sorta, could've, lets-look-at-this-in-the-parlance-of-our-times statement to add to it. Charles Bukowski was a fucker. I remember sitting in the Mu-Meson Archive, a loft in Sydney found just off Parramatta Road that plays obscure films, and watching a series of interviews with Bukowski. In one of them, he was sitting with his wife, Linda, answering questions, laughing, and having a good time. Then she says something that he doesn't like. I'm not sure what, now. I just remember watching as Bukowski's face changed. As the good humour drained out of it. He turned to his wife. He started yelling at her.

Calling her a bitch. Telling her that she was a lying slut of a bitch. Leaning back on the couch he starts to kick her. *Bitch!* Kick, kick. *Slut!* Kick, kick. As the cameras roll, he kicks and verbally abuses her until, crying, she flees the room.

Family – In the weeks after the funeral, Dad's parents told Mum that if she went back to work, she could expect no help from them. Tall, severe people, they were strict Catholics, and in the 80s that meant threatening your daughter in-law with financial abandonment, a threat they made good on. Mum wasn't so surprised. Uncles and aunts disappeared into the Australian outback, and Xmas cards would come from them, and phone calls, once or twice a year. One uncle lived on the outskirts of Sydney, and he was always available to help, when Mum asked, but she said that after a while that it felt like she was his charity case. Ten years ago, Dad's parents changed the writing on his grave, and afterwards, rang Mum, and told her the new words.

Factotum – Yet, for all that Charles Bukowski was an asshole, and someone who I would have trouble being friends with in real life, I admire his body of work without conflict. It is honest, raw, fearless and, at times, funny. *Pulp*, Bukowski's final novel, and which is dedicated to bad writing, is one of the most hilarious books I have ever read. No matter what you say about the man, Charles Bukowski the author was, at all times, passionate in his work. It is the defining quality of his writing and I do not believe that you can read any of Bukowski's work, even the minor pieces (and there are a lot of minor pieces) without seeing that passion. It is that passion that I admire. And it is through that passion that I have learnt to distinguish the work of the author from the life that he or she has lived, or is living.

Friends – They say that you can pick and choose your friends, but not your family. They are wrong.

FAQ –

- Do you always wear black?
- Why do you always wear black?
- Are you really bald?
- Are you really a doctor?
- How much money do you make?
- Is that really your penis?

G

Godless, A Dialogue –

I got a call from Mum today.

I bet that was fun.

Don't be an asshole. Not all mums can be like yours, you know.

That's true, but your mum has that special Christian insanity.

Don't say that.

What was she calling about then?

Children born in sin.

Greene, Graham – In his final interview, the great novelist Graham Greene described the United States as the world's new dictator. He died in 1991.

Godless, A Dialogue –

I like your mum right enough until she breaks out the God shit.

It's just that she believes in something.

She can believe in whatever she wants, so long as I don't have to do so.

She doesn't—

Just wait.

Table for two?

Thanks.

...

...

...

Yeah, thanks.

Look, Mum just has concerns.

That's all. It's just that the concerns come from her belief.

You know, I believe in things, too.

You're agnostic.

So?

Believing you'll figure it out when you die isn't having faith.

She was talking about dead children again, wasn't she?

Don't you ever wonder what'll happen if we die?

That's got nothing to do with your Mum.

I don't want to argue about Mum, okay?

Just tell me.

I don't think about death. It's fucking morbid.

You're a fucking morbid guy, B.

...

What?

What's the point of this?

I'm thinking of going back to church.

Gibson, Ross – In his book *Seven Versions of an Australian Badlands*, Ross Gibson presents a theory that land can become tainted by its history, and that if that history is negative, become a cultural badland. This area, be it a city, a stretch of road, a neighbourhood, whatever, really, becomes so tainted by the violence of its past that it has no other identity, affecting individuals so that they actively think of the area in a negative way before entering it. This means that when they enter a badland, they find things in the area that support the preconceived notion, and that anything which does not fit the "narrative" of the badland is rejected.

Godless, A Dialogue –

You haven't said anything about it.

I'm trying to think what I want to eat. I'm looking at all the dead things.

At the really, really dead things.

Something ought to have died for me tonight.

Don't be like that.

What do you want me to say, G?

You want to go to church, I'm not going to stop you. I'll even support it. I'm not going to rag on you because you want to do something.

But you don't like it.

I don't like a lot of shit.

Don't give me that.

...

Just tell me.

Fine.

I *don't* like it.

I don't like organised religion. I don't like the goals of organised religion. I don't like organisations, actually, but a room full of people who believe the same thing and who're trying to save their souls just gives me the shits. Inevitably they're going to think my soul needs saving, and my soul is just fine.

There are nice churches out there.

So? Religion is just laws on how to live, and they're not even consistent. People in religion break their own rules all the time—I don't see no Catholic church marching for peace. All I hear them telling me
is that gay people are evil and contraceptives make God cry. Sure, you might find a nice, progressive church, but it's just the same

old shit dressed in fashionable ideals.

And—

You're tirading.

—*And* I don't care.

Let's say those people are right. Let's say gay people are evil and wrong. So they all go to Hell. Wave goodbye. And because we're all nice straight people, we get into Heaven. That means I spend my afterlife with people who were fucking bigots. Fuck them, G.

I'd rather get myself reincarnated, or shoved into Hell, or whatever else choices there are.

I mean, do you really want to spend time with them?

No.

I think of those bigots, and I think of J, who is the most loveliest,
nicest guy, and I think, how can you hate someone
for how they're born? How could you think they were evil?
I hate people like that.

Then why bother with the church thing?

...

Come on. What is it?

I just want to feel safe.

Global Badland – American soldiers play music in their tanks. Personal soundtrack to a private first person shooter. Palestinian boys and girls strap home-made bombs to themselves. They walk out of cities ravaged by bombing and into diners that have been blown up twice. Israel drops bombs signed by eleven year old girls. Small rockets burst across the border from Lebanon and punch into buildings. A car is fire bombed in France by white men. An Indian father honour kills his fifteen year old daughter in Britain. She was pregnant to a white boy. Two British males kick an Indian man to death in the cubicle of a bar. In Germany a man eats another man. The Eaten agrees to it so long as they share his penis. It is flambéed. In America, four Police Officers shoot one African immigrant forty six times. He was at the door to his apartment complex. None of the officers are found guilty. A mother is beaten to death by her daughter in New Zealand. The girl uses a brick in a stocking. A film is made years later. Men and women and children gather in dirty refugee camps around the world. They are fleeing Iraq. They are fleeing Iran. They are fleeing war. They are fleeing hate. They are fleeing. They pay to get onto an ancient fishing trawler in Vietnam. The media tells us they are the rich refugees. Cramped, hot, desperate, they cross the ocean in ancient, decaying boats. They are heading for Australian shores. The Navy sinks their boat with machine guns. Later, the Prime Minister stands in a press conference and speaks about how these men and women hurled their children out of the boat to stop the Navy firing on them. They were trying to drown them, he says. Those monsters, he says. The obvious lie is revealed months later. Refugee camps in Australia grow bloated. Inside, men stitch their lips together in protest of the treatment they are receiving. They are not criminals, they say. They starve to prove it. They die with the media eye closed. The conservative party in Australia stays in power. They win each election with an ever gaining amount of support.

Godless, A Dialogue –

What have you got to be afraid of?

You know what I did today?

Puked into the Hello Kitty bucket?

I watched news channels. All day.I sat on that couch and
watched the news all day.
Do you know how many news channels are on cable? Five. Five
fucking channels from around the world. And there's five channels on
free to air. And I turned on the net and read sites there, and the net—
the net is worse, with its bloggers and independent
news services, because it shows you how much the ten channels on
TV are fucking sanitized.

You spent all day doing this?

All *day*.

It was war for oil, war for politics, war for fucking freedom. It's
violence here for wars out there. And then it is violence for just being
fucked up. Some guy cut another guy's dick off today!

And—

And people are afraid of losing jobs and money and petrol

...It was just so—

—so—

—Endless.

...

I didn't feel safe.

...

I don't know what to say.

43

I don't think you understand. You've never been out of the
country. Outside living in Brisbane this year,
you've spent your entire life in Sydney.

It's not a bad thing, it's just—
Look, I've been places.
I've been going to different countries since I was twelve.

I lived in Papa New Guinea for two years. I was an aid worker in
Africa for six months. I've been to America. I backpacked through
Europe. And—and in the sixteen years I've been doing this,
I have never felt afraid.
Never.

I was in Russia when I was twenty-two and I saw a guy get shot.
I was like three floors up. It was just one of those things. I'm standing
by the window. I'm drinking vodka—I mean, fuck, it's the middle of
the night and I'm drinking vodka and I look out my window and
there's this argument. Two guys yelling. And suddenly one of them
pulls out a gun—

—And he shoots the other dude.

You told me this.

I know.
But it hit me today—today it hit me that I didn't feel a fucking thing.
I wasn't afraid, I wasn't horrified, I wasn't—I wasn't anything. I just
watched. Later I said I was, but, but I wasn't.

It was like the world was giving me a spectacle to watch.
Some fucking moment of reality that I could tell everyone
about when I got back home.

You were drunk though.

Does that matter?

Every other day I turn on the TV and I don't feel anything. Dead
people in other countries. Starving kids I don't know. Parents who
leaves their kids. None of this has meant to me—I mean,
I know it's bad, I know I don't want it, but I don't feel it.

Today I felt it.
I could barely breathe.
It was—it was like it was suffocating me.

You think religion will make that go away?

...

No.
But what else can I do?

Gaia Hypothesis – The Gaia Hypothesis believes that all living
organisms should be considered part of the one living organism, and
that this one mass organism can alter the environment of the planet
as is necessary to survive. The theory is intended to promote global
responsibility. When I asked, none of my friends had heard of it.

Godless. A Dialogue –

I don't know what the answer is, G.

**I don't think religion's going to solve it, though. I mean, people fight
over religion more than any fucking thing in the world.**

I know.

It's just...

I dunno.

Hey, you know what?

You can bring about world peace?

We'll cancel the cable channels.

What?

The problem is clearly that we watch the news.

I mean, if we didn't watch the news, we'd never know about this shit.
So we'll cancel the cable. We've kill the net. We'll even toss
the TV out of the window. We'll throw it at a cripple.
One of them with the metal crutches. We'll take him out and then
steal his crutches and have sword fights.

...

Come on, you know you want it.

You're such an idiot.

Least you're laughing.

You're such a cunt sometimes.

It's why you love me baby.

I should feel more ashamed.

The little bit you have is more than enough.

You ready to order?

H

Hell –

High School – I spent six years in Pendle Hill High School. I would like to say that my mother and I put a lot of effort into this choice, but the truth is, the High School was up the road from the Primary School I attended. At the end of 1988, ninety percent of the students from Toongabbie Public School ended up in Pendle Hill High. If they were male, they wore grey and white. If female, white and brown. It

47

was—and still is—an ugly school. There are four blocks that look like thick guard towers, each of which are connected by a concrete walkway that formed one long walkway around the whole complex, forcing it into an enclosed square. On the walls spikes and barb wire stop people from climbing in after hours. Beneath the spikes are large iron gates that are closed after roll call at 8.55 am each day. Outside the gates are fields that aren't well kept, and which stretch to the back of houses or the bus bay. In class, you could look out a window, and see the emptiness, and wonder what it would be like to be leaving, instead of stuck in the ugly brown rooms listening to the drone of sanitized learning. If you think this description is rather similar to that of a prison... Well, you're not wrong.

Heterosexuality – My sexual preference is for females. When you add it to the fact that I am a white Australian, and that I'm male, I am the dominant Western form. I will never be asked to represent anyone in any official capacity within Australia. No media outlet will ask me to be the spokesperson for white people. No one will request that I represent straight people at a meeting. And no one will ask me to prepare a list of issues that men would like addressed in the workplace. Until I open my mouth, no one will discriminate against me at all. Ridiculous, really.

HIV/AIDS – Alive and Well is an organisation that believes that there has been no scientific proof that HIV causes AIDS. According to them, all the epidemiological and microbiological evidence taken together proves that HIV cannot cause AIDS (or any other illness, they argue). Alive and Well believe that this mass lie about AIDS can be traced back to Dr. Robert Gallo, the researcher responsible for revealing the connection between HIV and AIDS. They believe he did not have any evidence to support his claim, but was instead motivated by the financial rewards he would receive after revealing his theory, since he had, just that morning before his press conference, filed a patent for an antibody test that is now known as the AIDS Test. Alive and Well claims that after the New York Times ran the Gallo's press conference as their front page and announced the connection between HIV and AIDS—and thus presenting Dr. Gallo's findings as truth—they ensured that all other research into the possible causes of AIDS was brought to an "abrupt halt".

Hell – Eternal damnation is a strange concept, when you stop to think about it. Personally, what fascinates me, is how the descriptions of Hell are so focused on tactile sensations. This is not just limited to Dante and Milton, but also takes into account the many other fictional recreations, such as novels featuring Lucifer (or Satan or the Devil or however you wish to describe him), plays, films, and the endless parade of short fiction where a character ends up in Hell. By and large, the tactile is always there, even if the torture is on a mental level. Likewise, demons are described as creatures given over to their physical lusts: they want to fuck, they want to hurt, they want to consume. This dominance of tactile based Hells is particularly interesting because it links into the social sins that are placed upon society. To give in to our physical lusts is wrong. To be creatures of pure tactile sensation is to ignore spirituality, to ignore the soul, and to ignore the betterment of one's self.

Heaven – Yet, in opposition, while tactile pleasures are given to Hell, they are often ignored in Heaven. Generally speaking, God has no form that anyone can agree on, and angels are often portrayed as sexless figures, interested in the pursuit of knowledge and wisdom and not the carnal, base desires of their counterparts. There are, I know, other descriptions of Heaven, but rather than get into a long list of them, what fascinates me, is just how much Heaven, rather than existing as a reward, often functions as a description of a moral standard that the individual should live up to. No longer does Heaven and Hell exist as a reality, for I doubt they exist in any fashion that we could understand, but rather as a reflection of our own self. When you examine Heaven, you are being shown the cold, idealised version of a life that many are taught to aim for. It is free from conflict. It is simple. It is idyllic. It is love. It is without desire.

HIV/AIDS – According to statistics released by the AIDS Foundation, the world recognised body related to HIV/AIDS data, the rate of world wide infection of HIV/AIDS is between 1 to 1.3 percent. This percent is measured in the world's population of males and females between the ages of fifteen and forty-nine. The hardest hit area is the Sub-Saharan Africa, where it is believed that sixty percent of the world's HIV population exists. There, the infection rate is 6.6 to 8 percent. Since 1981, HIV/AIDS has been responsible for the deaths of more that twenty five million people.

Homosexuality – I am sitting in a café, on a date. In front of me is a cute, dark haired girl. She is wearing black and red, and the red is even in her hair. In the middle of eating, she begins talking about her faith, and how important it is. She tells me that homosexuality was wrong. She says that God had made a man and a woman. That is it. That is why homosexuality is wrong. Her bigotry is that strong. After finishing my meal, I leave, and tell her I won't call.

High School – In the six years I was at Pendle Hill High School, I never saw a brand new text book. In year eight, I saw a lot of porn. A guy I knew made his own porn film in year nine. There was a lot of alcohol. Not so much drugs. You were either an alcohol school or a drug school, I decided, at one point. Pendle Hill was an alcohol school. Alcohol wasn't my thing, however; it never has been. There was also a lot of Christianity, and that wasn't my thing either. The school band was a Christian Rock Band, which even then was unbelievably lame, but it was all the school had. They called themselves True Foundation. I tried not to speak to the band, but they were in half my classes in the final years, so it was unavoidable. Outside Christians, I knew a handful of guys who carried knives daily. One guy wore army boots just for that. I saw one gun, at the back of a field, in year ten. Most weeks, there was a fight. The library had less books in it than I personally own right now. I did assignments, sometimes. Homework never. I paid school fees once, in year seven. I did manage to watch a lot of cartoons, however. And then, after six years, I left Pendle Hill High School with a mark of 36.45, which meant that 64.55 percent of the NSW population had scored higher than me in the final year of exams. When I got the letter, I was even a little shocked, the result of being slightly arrogant and having coasted throughout High School with solid marks. Of my friends, only C got a lower mark than me. He got the Triangle, which meant that his mark was 15 <. He did better than me in some of his exams and spent a good six months complaining about how they couldn't even be bothered to give him a real mark. The problem, of course, was that neither of us did any of the socially respected subjects like physics, math, or biology. Even if you failed those subjects, you were scaled up in, or that's how it was back in 1994. Anyhow: it didn't really matter. The next day C and I went and signed up for unemployment. Three months later, Pendle Hill High School was listed by the NSW Board of Education as a Disadvantaged School.

Heaven –

I

Identity – I grew too quickly. That is what the Doctor said. I was five and had not yet finished growing, but I had already grown too quickly. My muscles could not keep up. That was why I walked on the balls of my feet. I still do. In boots, it is barely noticeable. In sneakers I slide and slouch. I'm rarely barefoot around people I do not know. In addition, my feet are pigeon toed. When the Doctor told me I grew too fast, I was tall, thin, messy red hair and freckles. I filled out as I got older. It's a mix of muscle and fat now. I use weights. I walk regularly. I'm lazy. I like junk. I spend most of my day in front of a computer. I was grunge as a teenager: flannelette shirts, ripped jeans, sneakers, band t-shirts, all of it a few sizes too big. I still wear clothes too big. No logos. I hate being a walking billboard. It is black, mostly. Bit of red, bit of white. At thirteen the dentist said the roof of my mouth was too small. I had a cross bite. He put a plate at the roof of my mouth and each night, Mum would reach in with a small, metal key, and turn it once. I had bad acne at fifteen. Mum took me to a skin specialist. He put me on drugs. They made me quiet and sullen, or so the packaging warned. The pills did cause puss to ooze from my nails, however. For over a year I had Band-aids around my fingers. My hair started receding when I was seventeen. The irony was I that I was covered in hair everywhere else. I could grow a beard at sixteen. I shaved my head at nineteen. I haven't had hair for ten years. Not one person has said that these solutions to my various imperfections was wrong.

Image - In 1988, Cindy Jackson wrote a wish list: *I wanted:*

Larger, less tired-looking eyes

A small, feminine nose

High cheekbones

Fuller, better-shaped lips

Perfect white teeth

A smaller, more delicate jaw and chin

To have just the one chin

To eradicate premature facial wrinkles and acne scarring

A flawless, unlined complexion

A defined waistline and flat stomach

To lose my love handles, saddle bags and cellulite

Thinner thighs and slimmer knees

To get rid of flab left over from being fifty pounds

overweight in the 70s

Not to have to wear a life time of hardship etched on my face

Identity – I was an extra in the film *Footy Legends.* I got the job like this: I was walking down the main street of Parramatta with C, and a skinny white guy with a clipboard and a digital camera stopped us. Were we interested in being in a film? he asked. He promised us money and food. We agreed without asking any details, and he took our photos, and said he would call back. A month later I was called, but C was not. He bitched about that until I told him why I was hired, the day after the job. It wasn't until I showed up in St. Mary's at six in the morning that I started to figure out why it had been me who was offered work, and not C. Standing next to toothless men, men with beards down to their chests, women with too much makeup and too much hair dye, men who were covered in bumps and lumps, women with tattoos, men who were fat, men who were warn down, and one midget, I realised I had been hired to fill out the freak scene. A big mean guy in black. C is too normal looking. Too non-descriptive. So I was their choice and, in most of the scenes, I was put next to the midget. We sat in the stadium and pretended to eat and talk when the camera rolled. When the camera was off, we talked for real. He was a bit of an asshole, actually.

Image – Cindy Jackson began the alterations to her body with an inheritance. The money from a dead relative—a mother, a father, a grandfather, an uncle, I am not sure—allowed Cindy to begin the slow murder of the body they had known. It took sixteen years and nine operations (and an unspecified number of procedures such as light chemical peels, permanent makeup, cosmetic dentistry, and filler injections). When the inheritance money ran out, Cindy took out loans, had cash advances, and used credit cards. Without the money of the dead, she was forced to use money she did not have to create an image that did not yet exist.

Identity – 'No one would ever guess you were a genius,' R says to me. We have just had sex, but it hasn't gone well. Her hand got caught on the door. I slipped on the sheets. The condom broke. She isn't on the pill. The phone is ringing. It is my phone. I have no idea where it is.

Image – The language used to describe Cindy Jackson is often harsh and critical. Society doesn't admire overt demonstrations of cosmetic surgery like hers. Instead, we're happy when starlet lips are plumped on the quiet. When wrinkles are smoothed without so much as a mention. When hair is coloured so regularly that it is natural. But in many ways, Cindy is more admirable than the people who secure the little fixes, because she, through the transformation of her self, has exercised full control over her body. No one can question her possession of self. She owns what we all own from birth: a body. She has every right to chip, break, cut, implant, and deplant across her form. We should admire the amount of self-determination she has shown. The discipline she has demonstrated. We should be critical not of her, because her changes, so public, show the extent to which beauty has become artificial; instead, we should save our criticisms for the culture that urges these changes to be hidden and that tells us that the artificial beauty we admire and aspire towards is, in fact, natural.

Identity – Being used as scene scum in *Footy Legends* did not do me any good. Intimidating, bald, the friend of a midget: Ben Peek, for hire. It dug under my skin. It was as if I had been picked off the street and shown, in sudden clarity, how the world viewed me. I had heard it before from strangers, from students, from the parents of students, and from the families of girls I dated; but it had never dug as deep as it did on that film set. The problem was not that I disliked how a stranger had seen me, but because the other "scum" on the set were, with the exception of the midget, the nicest people when I met them. Laid back, easy going, fun. But I viewed myself as being better than them. When it came to judging on images, I did exactly what had been done to me, and viewed them as scum, as being *beneath* me, and the realisation that I did this just as someone had done it to me dug into my psyche. The insight was not one that I enjoyed.

Image – In an interview, Cindy Jackson responded to those who criticised what she had done, saying, 'I grew up being criticised for everything from my big nose to the way I dressed. Now I get criticised for doing something about it!'

Identity

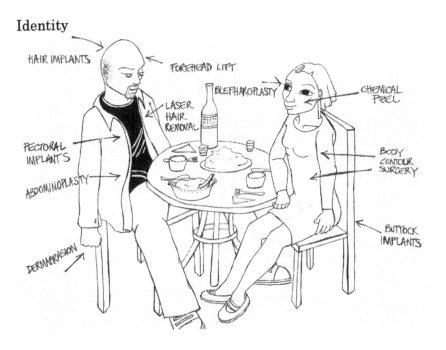

Image – I admire Cindy, but at the same time, I find myself caught in a moral complexity about her. With her artificial beauty, Cindy has been able to make a career for herself and, as she did her body, she has fashioned a Z-grade level of fame that has allowed to her to earn a living fronting charities, working as a model, having small acting parts, and fronting a band called Dolls. With money, she has bought her beauty, and because she has not ended up as a pale, ugly man whose nose breaks, and who is rumoured to sleep in an oxygen chamber and molest children, she has been allowed to step out of the person that she was. Now existing in a state of unrealness, she has been rewarded. She has become the extreme representation of a culture that alters the photos of models, uses makeup to hide pimples on teen actors, and injects botox into the faces of aging men and women around the world. I cannot respect her because she further perpetrates the myth that there is a perfect beauty, that idea that there is one look to aspire too and which, from beauty pageants to diet guides, men and women of all ages around the world must compare themselves with. As much as I dislike that, I am not free from it, either. I am aware of my own imperfections: the handles, the lack of tone, the lack of hair, and the many other ways that I don't equal what is considered beautiful. I see it and I tell myself it doesn't matter. But for all that I tell myself that, when I look at an image of Cindy Jackson, I think that she is beautiful, and for all that she shows what a terrible lie beauty has become, my desires do not care.

J

Jesus – I am standing on the streets of Stanmore, in Sydney, with J. I have a camera. It is dark, wet, but not really cold. J begins walking up the road. He is dressed in white robe with a golden rope tied around his waist. He looks like Jesus. He is meant to look like Jesus. He is pretending to break into cars dressed as Jesus. I am taking photos of him. It is my idea, part of a project I am working on, but J has always liked to dress up like Jesus. When I brought up the idea, he agreed without hesitation. He already had a Jesus costume. He reminds me of the fact that in year six, he forced me to join the Christian School Group so that he could be Jesus in the yearly play. I was a centurion.

Jesus and Mary Chain, The – In 1987, the Jesus and Mary Chain released *Darklands*. It is the near perfect album for breakups and cold, wet days. I found the album twelve years after its release, the same year the Jesus and Mary Chain officially broke up.

Justice – On the 28th April, 1996, Martin Bryant walked into the Port Arthur café, *The Broad Arrow*, and killed twenty-two people. Nineteen of these people were killed from shots to the head, though Bryant had no background proficiency with weapons. In fact, Bryant himself was reported to have an IQ of 66, and drew a State disability pension due to this. In *The Broad Arrow*, he killed twenty-two people after firing twenty-nine rounds from the AR-15 he was carrying. The

AR-15 is a lightweight, magazine-fed, auto-loading rifle. Once outside the café, he proceeded to kill another thirteen men, women, and children. He injured thirty-seven others. Eventually caught, he is currently serving a life sentence without the possibility of parole in Risdon Prison, having received no consideration due to his mental disability in sentencing. Showing rare taste, or knowing that they cannot portray a mentally retarded man on television or in print as a mass murderer, the media has conducted no interviews with Bryant who, since entering prison, has been on suicide watch, and kept in isolated cells. In 1996, when Bryant could legally purchase the two semi automatic machine guns used in the killings, Tasmanian State law listed sex between two consenting males as punishable by up to twenty-five years in prison. Within weeks of the Port Arthur Massacre, as it is now known, politicians changed the gun laws in Tasmania, though gun related murders were a statistical anomaly. The anti-homosexual law, in comparison, was overturned in 1997 after Amnesty International brought worldwide condemnation to the State. It was not until 2004 that Tasmania legally recognised homosexual relationships.

Job Interview – The man in front of me is asking if I have a criminal record. He is American, a brown haired, white skinned, neatly dressed American. I have applied for a job in a new fast food chain called Chili's. I am seventeen. I tell him no. He says, 'Don't worry, you can tell me the truth. I won't hold it against you.'

Judgment – I argue with people about the nature of justice all the time. For many, a sentencing is about the punishment, about the suffering. Criminals are removed from society for a reason, they explain. They are evil. They do not deserve the freedoms that innocent people have. While I do admit that there are times when I am happy for particularly harsh crimes to be met with equally harsh punishment, I do not think that the nature of justice should be about inflicting suffering on an individual. It is rare for a crime to be committed in a vacuum of understanding: a man or woman does not wake up one morning and, for no particular reason, drive a knife into their sleeping partner beside them. Rather, I view justice to be about understanding the reasons for the action; and I view prison as a tool for reformation. Like Michel Foucalt, I believe that prison, along with schools and hospitals, are meant to be part of a social wide project that transforms individuals for better. I am aware, however, that there is a larger issue outside this: just whose image are people being transformed into. It is a question I often ask when I'm teaching.

Jobs, First – The first job I ever paid taxes at was in a cinema. I was hired as an usher, but four months after that, the Media Arts and Alliance Union allowed for the projectionist trade to be abolished. This meant, firstly, that the per-screen hourly pay rate that projectionists had been earning was slashed, and secondly, it meant that ushers could be trained to run films, and that was all. I was one of the first, and that meant I picked up a lot of the side skills, such as how to repair wiring and replace parts in the head of the machine. Because of this, I ended up working for four years as a "projectionist" in a heritage listed cinema building. It had been painted pink. I ran three screens. The average eight-hour shift involved me threading film through a projector every two hours, once per screen. I was quick. I could do each in under a minute.

Judges – I enter the courthouse with C. We are twenty-three. He has been called as a witness in an assault case. Since I have never been to a courthouse, I agree to go out of curiosity. At the Parramatta Court House, the two Police Officers on the front desk make us walk through the metal detector. We join the line to do so. Once inside, C sits and waits. After a while, I get bored and go looking for something interesting. I want murder. I've seen black and white episodes with Raymond Burr in *Perry Mason*. There must be that somewhere. But the courtrooms are mostly empty, and those that have people in them are not very dynamic. As a spectator sport, I decide, the law is boring. In addition, there is a sign instructing me to bow to the judge as I enter and leave. How curious, I think, but do not bow. As if you would bow to a stranger. Finally, I end up in a courtroom where a Chinese man, about my age, is being sentenced for assault. This is not the

calling of witnesses that C is sitting through, but the climax.
Excellent. I take a seat up the back, but only the Chinese guy's family
is present. I feel a little uncomfortable; it occurs to me that I am
really just invading their private moment for my own selfish
amusement. I sit there, dressed in black, shaved head, scuffed Docs,
and headphones round my neck. I am obviously not part of the family.
I shouldn't be there. But I wait. The Chinese guy's white lawyer is
looking through files. I keep waiting. The white Lawyer goes up to the
white Judge. They talk for a bit. I continue to wait. They talk a bit
more. Then the white Judge tells the Chinese guy and his family that
the white lawyer has forgotten his file. Then he sentences the
Chinese guy to six months in jail.

Jobs, A Dialogue –

Speaking of mothers, I called mine today.

How is she?

She's fine.

In fact, she got a new rescue dog.

Again? Isn't this like the fourth one?

Sixth.

I swear, she gets them, and in two to three months, they get terminal
illnesses, she spends thousands on them, and then they die within
the year.

It's fucking tragic.

She's going to have a little line of urns at the door
when we visit next.

The weird thing is, I grew up with two dogs that lived to be sixteen, and who were never sick except at the end.

She has got some strange karma going on there.

Did she say anything else?

...

What?

You know, don't you?

Know what?

Don't—

Shit.

I hate it when two of you talk behind my back.

I didn't know she was going to talk about it, I was just—

Worried.

We're going to need more money.

You think I don't know that?

I don't know. Sometimes I think no.

You hate work—no, that's not it. I'm not being fair. You hate employment. You've never had a full time job. You've either had the equivalent in two or three, or you've made the money for the month with a bit of freelancing or short story, and you can make that stretch.

63

Stretch so much.

And I think you're going to try and stretch it still.

You make good money.

It's not enough for three.

...

Don't go silent.

What do you want me to say?

I get it. We need cash. Specifically, I need cash.

I could be earning three times as much as I do, I know that. I did the degrees. But I *don't* want to spend forty hours a week at a job I don't care for.

I *don't* want to spend ten hours a week traveling to and from it.

I *don't* want to waste my life doing something that means absolutely nothing to me.

Sometimes you got to do things you don't like.

Who decided that was a fucking rule?

That's such a fucking elitist rule, and people who don't have to do that put it out there. You don't have to do it, because you're doing what you love.

It doesn't even occur to you that you could go find a job that pays more, because you're doing what you want, but me, because I *can't* make money doing what I love, I got to do something I don't like.

You're being childish.

I'm *not*.

...

...

...

I'm thinking about getting a dip ed.

Teaching?

Joy Division – The British band Joy Division were named after groups of women who were used as sex slaves in Nazi concentration camps as depicted in the novel *House of Dolls,* written by Yehiel De-Nur. De-Nur, however, published the novel under the name Ka-Tzetnik 135633. In Hebrew, "Ka-Tzetnik" means "Concentration Camper" and the number that followed his name was the camp number that De-Nur was given during his time imprisoned. After the band had selected the name, they were accused of insensitivity to those that had suffered at the hands of the Nazis, and were even said to be neo-Nazis themselves, a claim that they strongly denied. After Ian Curtis' suicide in 1980, however, the surviving members of the band named themselves New Order, in reference to one of Hitler's speeches where he promised a new order of the Third Reich.

Judas – In Christian mythology, it is said that Judas betrayed Jesus for thirty pieces of silver. That is, if he existed. There is some confusion about Judas' place in the Bible, as it is argued by some that he is in fact Saint Jude or Saint Thomas, though this is not a popular theory. However, early Christian writings are also rumoured to spend very little time on Judas, and what time they do spend on him does not paint him as the traitor that the Church now does. However, if you are to believe in Judas as a betrayer, the common theory is that he betrayed Jesus as an act of free will. His betrayal shows that Jesus never forced any man or woman to follow him. They were free to come and go as they wished. In Judas' case, he was free to betray for a small box of silver. Later, on that land that he purchased, he fell down and shattered, his bowels bursting across the ground. Which is certainly an interesting fate for the man who was meant to show us that we all have free will.

K

Kujau, Konrad – Konrad Kujau, born in 1938, and dead in 2000, was the forger who created the sixty-two volumes that comprised the *Hitler Diaries*.

Killer – I grew up in a room full of guns. Shooting was Dad's hobby, and he had a big wooden cabinet made so he could store his rifles and pistols at home safely. There wasn't much room in the house, so they ended up with me. I suppose he thought guns were more appropriate for a boy's room, than for a girl's. Behind the glass and locks, he threaded a thick chain through the trigger guards, and locked it with a padlock the size of his hand; he kept the bolts of the rifles hidden in the garage with the equipment he used to make bullets. All in all, it was all pretty safe. Yet, before most kids reached metal work classes in High School, I had learnt to boil lead and pour it into moulds for bullets. I knew how much powder to put into a copper casing. I knew what the satisfied crunch sound was when the bullet and casings were put together. I thought it was fun, except when, on Saturday mornings, he would take me out to shooting ranges. I would rather have been at home, watching *Transformers*, which was on at that time.

Khouri, Norma – Norma Khouri is a Jordanian woman currently living in exile in Australia and the author of the memoir, *Forbidden Love*, published in 2003. In the book, Khouri claimed that she and a friend, Dalia, opened a unisex hairdressing salon in Jordan in the early nineties. During that time, Dalia pursued a relationship with a Christian man, Michael, but once Dalia's family discovered the illicit love, her father stabbed her to death. In response, Khouri, with the help of Michael, fled the country, writing her book in internet cafes throughout Athens, before ending up in Queensland. In 2004, it was revealed that the book was nothing but fiction. During the time that Khouri is reported to have lived in Jordan, she was, in fact, living in Chicago with her husband and two children. Furthermore, the unisex hairdressing salon could not have existed by law at the time, and there is no public record off it having existed. Attacks on Khouri have centred on her stereotypical portrayal of Middle Eastern families and her complete inability to represent the area or people realistically. In addition to this, *Forbidden Love* is reported to have seventy-three errors or exaggerations in it. It was ranked fifty-five in the annual Angus and Robertson one hundred favourite books list, and continues to be published by Random House.

K is for Sister – My sister was born nineteen months after I was, but we are not very close. During High School, she arranged for a group of male friends to attack me after school, but due to my sister's limited description of me as a 'Fat guy with red hair,' they ended up attacking the wrong guy. *That* fat, red haired guy got two broken ribs. Nowadays, we simply have nothing in common. We keep in contact through our mother, or we'll call when it is coming up on Mum's birthday or Xmas, or when she needs something. Likewise, for our grandparents. However, she once threw an ex-girlfriend of mine out of a bar she was working in because she had broken up with me, so I suppose that says something for sibling affection.

Koestler, Arthur – I consider the final lines of *Darkness at Noon* flawless. It is not just that it is a well-written line, because there have been well written lines in many novels. Rather, these final lines are, instead, able to convey the tragedy, the thematic politics, and the dark humour of Koestler's novel, summing it up with such a succinct, perfect thrust into the subconscious that when one lays the book down, one knows exactly what one has read. However, while it is correct to praise Koestler, he is not responsible for the novel being written in English, and therefor it is incorrect to acknowledge him fully for the book. Daphne Hardy translated *Darkness at Noon* from Russian, and it is she, I believe, who must also be acknowledged when one talks about the flawlessness of the novel. A translation is not the simple swapping of one word from another, but rather the careful reconstruction of a novel from one language to that of a new language. It is, in effect, rewritten, reborn, remade. In English, it was not Arthur Koestler who provided perfection, but Daphne Hardy.

Kindred – When my father's father died, I did not go to his funeral. I had not seen him for ten years. I did not go to see him in the hospital as he lay there dying, even though it was requested. I refused to see his wife, my father's mother, my grandmother, at the time, and I still refuse. I have five uncles that I do not see. Six aunts purposefully made absent. One of them is my mother's sister, who refuses to visit her parents. There are eight cousins I do not know. Three have gotten married. I was invited to two weddings, went to neither. One has a child. I do, however, see one cousin, occasionally. I see my sister slightly more. Mum's parents monthly. Mum every week. If I have more family, I don't know about it.

Khan, Rahila – Khan is the author of a slim paperback collection, *Down the Road, Worlds Away*, which contained twelve stories about Asian girls and Caucasian boys, and which was lauded, in 1987, as a breakthrough for feminist literature. Like most authors who are not what they claim to be, Khan never granted interviews, and never published an author photo. It was not until an agent agreed to represent Khan that she came out of hiding, and revealed herself to be the very male, very white, Reverend Toby Forward, from the Church of England. Forward was attacked for misrepresentation on a number of levels, but due to the small size of the book, and its limited audience, managed to go on publishing children's fiction under his own name.

Kiss – I am ten. She is eight. I push my tongue into her mouth, but her teeth are in the way, and she pulls away in disgust. Indignant, she asks me what I am doing. I tell her I saw it on TV, but I lie, I lie.

Kinship – I can remember the moment when I decided that I would not see my extended family anymore: Xmas '92. Mum drove my sister and I out to a farm in Windsor, to take part in the Peek family lunch. It was warm—in the background was a faint orange light. A part of the Blue Mountains was on fire. It always is in December. Mum has organised gifts for all the aunts and uncles and cousins, spending more money than she should; especially since the gifts given back were always cheap, disposable stuff. It sounds petty now, but there was always a quality difference in the gifts given out and the gifts received. The year before, the only cousin my age, had been given a watch by our grandparents. I got a book. It was second hand. The price was still written in pencil on the front page: *$2.50*. The watch was new. At any rate, there was a big lunch organised, and after the lunch everyone gave their presents. That was the ritual. My three uncles and one aunt went first, because they had organised a group present for their mother and father: a giant, big as you could find at the time, television. It had a card attached to the front, telling them that they would all be going away together up the coast. In the excitement that followed, I distinctly remember looking at Mum, who was, now, standing in the doorway of the kitchen. A tiny, brown haired woman with a soft, British accent, she stood outside the circle of their family, clutching her carefully wrapped gift tightly, and waiting to give it to her in-laws. Death had made her the outsider. The widow. The visible reminder of a dead son and brother. To the Peek family, she was an afterthought, a belated apology, a last minute invite and, standing in that doorway, standing, watching, she knew it. She knew that she was not part of this family, that she was not wanted, even; but she suffered it so that her children could be connected to it.

Kujau, Petra – Petra is the grand niece of the forger Konrad Kujau. She was arrested in 2006 for selling forgeries of Konrad's own forgeries.

L

Lust – D and I are walking through the grass basin that feeds off the concrete creek running behind our houses. It is school break. In six weeks, we begin High School. Before that, we will spend Summer exploring the long, dry, sun yellowed grass and shallow, stagnant pools of water in the basin. The skeletons of giant telephone towers watch over us. D, more adventurous than I, climbs up to the barb wire one day. But today, in the dry grass, hidden beneath an old oil drum (there are grey and brown featureless factory blocks around the basin) we find a stash of magazines. They are filled with naked women. These naked women have firm breasts. They have seductive eyes. They are nineteen, twenty, older, we don't know. Some have pubic hair. Some do not. They are beautiful. They are naked. They stare out of the pages with desire. More than anything else, D and I know that these women want a pair of twelve year old boys more than they could want any male in the world. Quickly, we divide up the stash and, with it hidden under shirts, head back home.

Lady – I do not use the word lady. To me, it is a word caught up in class and racial descriptions, and I am uncomfortable with it. When I have encountered a white woman who called herself a lady, it always remind me of a Jane Austen novel; I inevitably think of rich, white women who sit around drinking tea and having conversations about men, marriage, and other such things. It could very well be that all of Austen's novels are not about sitting around and drinking tea and discussing marriage, but I read *Emma*, and that was enough for me.

The word lady was destroyed forever. However, when the word lady is used in relation to non-white women, I connect it with a class driven attempt to identity with the first meaning, and it has thus became laden with a sense of class and race and an ugliness that I cannot remove. Because of this, the world lady has fallen into disuse around me, and it lies there, in my head, gathering dust.

Larter, Ali – American model/actor Ali Larter was the image for Allegra Coleman, a beautiful model turned actor who was invented by Martha Sherrill in 1996, and first revealed in *Esquire*. Sherrill's plan with Coleman was to satirize the celebrity articles that appeared about new stars, where they discussed not what the new model or actor was doing, or if she had an opinions, but rather focused entirely on her relationship with a celebrity, the nude photos that the paparazzi had taken, and her previous sexual partners. Sherrill was attempting to show just how fixated we had become on the female form and its sexual interactions to the point that it made everything else secondary, even reality. The editor of *Esquire*, however, killed the hoax shortly after that issue went to print. Recently, Sherrill has written a fictional novel featuring Coleman.

Lolita – Lolita is the sexual fetish term for a girl who is below the legal age of consent (or who looks as if she is below the age of consent) but who is sexually desired by men and women. In response, the girl has a sexual appetite that has just awoken, and is being explored. A certain amount of wholesomeness must be maintained for it to work. In recent years, the lolita image has become one of the most commercial fetishes to trade off, with youth becoming an ever more important quality in the coding of the female body for sexual desire. Pop stars are the most obvious example of this: they are instructed by men and women older than them in the way to shape and move their body to mirror a sexuality that, according to press releases and agents, they have no awareness of, and no desire to explore. If any are found to be engaging in sexual actions, the lolita is considered tainted and her loss of purity destroys her apparent marketability.

Liddell, Alice – It is argued that Lewis Carroll, the author of *Alice in Wonderland*, was sexually attracted to young girls. Certainly, he enjoyed taking photos of naked young girls. The girl Alice Liddell, who was not the inspiration for Alice, though many mistakenly believe so, was said to be his favourite. There are no surviving nude photos of Liddell, if there ever were any, though Carroll's diaries of the years that he and the girl knew each other were destroyed by relatives, thus fueling speculation that some kind of relationship had taken place. There is a photo in which Liddell, aged seven, and dressed as a beggar that many point to in proving this. In it, Liddell has her back against the wall. Her shoulder is bare. On her face is a look caught somewhere between bemusement and desire, a confused hint of adolescent innocent colliding with the already existing desires of a man much older than her. The Liddell family eventually broke off their relationship with Carroll in 1863, when Alice was eleven. Her mother is to have believed the author an inappropriate suitor.

Lost Girls – In interviews for their new pornographic graphic novel, *Lost Girls*—which features underage girls having sex—author Alan Moore and artist Melinda Gebbie claimed that there was, in Western countries, a growing desire to police the sexual imagination.

Lolicon – Lolicon is the shortened version of the manga known as Lolita Complex. As the term Lolita did, Lolicon rose out of Vladimir Nabokov's novel, and referred to the sexual desire of girls below the age of consent. Lolicon, however, is one step beyond the lolita fetish, in that it actively shows young girls—the male equivalent is called shotacon—having sex with adults. Since it is artwork, and no real people are used, the girls are portrayed at the beginning stages of puberty, and cannot be mistake for being sixteen or older, even though the images are portrayed with the traditional banality that renders pornography ultimately unsatisfying. Lolicon books are available in bookstores and in newsstands in Japan, though in 2006, there was a call to outlaw the material.

Lords, Traci – Originally born Nora Louise Kuzma, the white

American actress Traci Lords began her career in pornography at the age of fifteen, modeling for *Penthouse*. A boyfriend who she lived with, and who posed as her stepfather in public, arranged for her to get fake IDs. At sixteen, Lords appeared in her first pornographic film, *What Gets Me Hot*, and in the following two years, appeared in over one hundred films, though she claims that over eighty were made from scenes either used or cut out of other films. She estimates that the total number of films she made before her eighteenth birthday was twenty. Lords fans, while unaware of her actual age, were attracted to her youthful appearance and the energy that went into her performances. To them, Traci Lords enjoyed her acting, to the point that many believed her authentic in her enjoyment of the scenes. Two days after her eighteenth birthday, she made her final, and only legal pornographic film, *Traci, I Love You*. Since then, Lords, still using her pornographic stage name, has appeared in a number of b-grade films, though her underage films remain the most popular.

Leave – At ten, I was attracted to girls my own age, girls younger, and girls older. Asked to articulate it, I would have had difficulties, but that does not make it untrue. At twenty-nine, able to articulate what it is that I desire, I am still attracted to girls my own age, girls younger, and girls older. The younger females are not ten, since I am attracted to the way girls curve, and I am drawn to girls who are witty, cynical, engaging—girls who can stimulate me intellectually— but they are not all over the age of eighteen. Statistically speaking, in twenty-nine years, I have been attracted to more teenage girls than I have been to women in their thirties. Will that remain true as I get older, or will it change? Will younger women lose their appeal? Will I desire only older women? Will desire leave altogether? Or will I be like Anthony Burgess who, throughout his life, engaged the services of a number of prostitutes including, most infamously, a twelve-year-old Tamil girl, to have sex with him?

Love – I was in love, once. Just once, mind. It is getting harder to remember now. The feelings I felt so strongly are disappearing and the girl I loved is no longer here.

M

Molestation – Between the ages of six and eleven. She had the same name as my mother.

Macleod, Fiona – In 1894, the author William Sharp published *Pharais, A Romance of the Isles*, under the name Fiona Macleod. Two books later, the Macleod audience had outstripped his own, and the books had begun to bring in money. At this point, Sharp created the personality of Fiona Macleod. He took much of the good elements that had been projected through her publications and began to write letters in her name, though he had his sister, Mary, rewrite them before they were mailed. Under his own name, he wrote letters promoting her. Publicly, he was sometimes her agent. Occasionally her cousin. Rarely, a lover. For eleven years he maintained this double life until, in 1905, he died, having never revealed the truth, and never been suspected. He said that to reveal the truth would be to lose the ability to write as Fiona Macleod; that it would block the internal channel he had to her work and, in effect, kill her. Also, he needed the money.

Memory – Your memory is a shrine. You know an event happened a certain way and you keep to it. It is your experience. Your knowledge. Your assurance. You tell your friends about things that happen to you. You learn to pause for a hint of the dramatic. You learn what lines get the best laugh. You learn which stories get the best response. Slowly, you begin to make your own mythology out of these memories. Occasionally, details slip through the crack. You do not quite remember right. A colour. A word. You recall poorly. Sometimes, you don't want to remember, so you do it on purpose. Your memories are not just a way to remember, a simple recall mechanism, but also become a way for you to commiserate with others, to commemorate those that have passed. Soon, you realise that you do not want your memories attacked. You will defend them. They are your temple. Your shrine. Your only consistent form of tangible evidence for your life lived. Without them, would you still be who you are?

Murder – I park near a red car. My car is also red. This won't become important until later, when the NSW Police Department has taped off the area around the two cars. Red car number one belongs to me. Red car number two belongs to a murderer who has just committed suicide in the shopping mall. A heavy set Police Officer will say to me, 'Which is your car?' and I will say, 'The red one.' But before that, as I leave the car park, two teenagers call out to me. I give them the finger. I can't quite make out what they're saying, so I figure they're trying to pick a fight. After I tell the Police I own a red car, the heavy set officer tells me that a body was discovered by two teenagers; the body's hands and feet had been tied up, and he has been thrown off the edge of the car park. He fell two floors and landed on his neck. The body lay like a tiny temple surrounded by shuddering air conditioners and wire fencing. But at that time, I walk past the teenagers and down the escalator, pleased at my response. Inside the mall, crowds of people have gathered near the railings. A girl mentions that a guy jumped over. This person is the driver of the other red car. The red murder car. More immediately, I learn that he fell four department store floors before landing on the hard tiles outside an ice cream parlour. Dead on impact. His body is hidden behind curtained walls and ceiling. As I walk past the curtains, I can see through the cracks. I see blood. I see a dead gold fish. That will never be explained. Next to the curtains, the ice cream parlour is still open. There is a line of people, buying ice cream.

McLuhan, Marshall – 'The book is a private confessional,' wrote Marshall McLuhan, who died on the final day of 1980. 'It provides a point of view.'

Mifune, Toshiro (Surrogate Father Figure #2) – In Japan, he was once chosen as the perfect representation of Japanese masculinity, but perhaps it was true no matter the race of the viewer. On the screen, Mifune is at turns rough, charming, worldly and knowledgeable; at other times quiet, introspective, a loner, violent, made vulnerable through his betrayals and weaknesses. For me, Mifune emerged from Akira Kurosawa's films, where, in *Yojimbo* and *Sanjuro*, he played the confident, lone samurai. A warrior who had his own rules. A man who did not concern himself with what others thought of him. A solitary figure that roamed where he pleased, did as he wanted, and answered to no one. A masculinity to admire.

Multiple Worlds Theory, A Dialogue –

You want to teach high school?

I don't want to teach it.

You don't think there's something wrong about the idea of a guy who hates employment becoming a high school teacher?

I'm planning to bond through hate.

That doesn't reassure me.

Hey, you're the one who says we need money. This is my idea. The least you could do is be supportive of it. Maybe in another world you are.

What?

It's that multiple worlds theory. An infinite number of worlds
stretched out, each made from an important choice we make.
Fuck, they might have a new one the moment you make a choice.

Maybe there's a world out there where I ate Coco Pops for breakfast.

So instead of coming to Brisbane, you stayed in Sydney?

Yeah. Things like that.

Do you think there's still a you in Sydney?

It's just a theory, and not real provable, either.

Are you telling me you don't want to be here?

What?

Answer the fucking question!

What the fuck are you on about?

You want to be back with no responsibility, is that it?

Did I say that?

You're one step away from it!

Lately, every fucking—

I get the feeling from you that you think you made
the wrong choice when you came up here.

You've got to be fucking kidding me.

No.

> No, I'm not. And if some little part of you that wants out,
> you fucking say, and you say it to me right now.

Mescal – I am in Bundaberg, up the coast of Queensland. I arrived on a small, propeller driven plane, sitting next to an Indian doctor who hadn't slept for two days. I stay at O and U's house. A new environment. A new thought. I can feel everything from the past six months fall away. It flakes. I am shedding skins. I haven't worn shoes for three days. My feet are dirty. I might be getting a tan. I swim in the ocean. Two days before I leave, I buy a bottle of Mescal. It has two worms in it. Worms for Lovers, the label tells me. I tell O that one is for her. I tell U the other one is for him. He agrees without pause. O, on the other hand, stares at the bottle for a good five minutes and, then, finally, quietly, tells me that there are worms in the alcohol. Worms do *not* belong in alcohol. She will *not*, she says, be eating dirty worms. *Not* even for love. I make sure to leave them the bottle when I go.

Malley, Ern – One of Australia's most widely known literary hoaxes. Ern Malley was a British immigrant in the 1920s who died at the age of twenty-five, but left behind a large, unpublished body of poetry, waiting to be found and published to acclaim as all unpublished poets are. In truth, Malley was the creation of James McAuley and Harold Stewart, both young poets at the time, and who decided that they would reveal the hollow nature of Australian literature with Malley's poems. They reportedly created the Malley poems in an afternoon, writing without conscious thought, and lifting phrases haphazardly from two dictionaries and a collection of Shakespeare's plays. They were purposefully making bad poetry and it was received as literature by one journal. Historically, it is argued that McAuley and Stewart's stunt had an adverse effect on the arts in Australia, and is said to have strengthened the conservative point of view about literature: that even the so called intellectuals publishing it do not know what they were on about, and that this work was being deliberately obscured for "common" people. Literature, the conservatives said, now defined as anything that stepped outside simple and traditional narratives, was the pursuit of those who believed themselves above the common people.

M is for Mother – My mother was meant to be named K, but her father decided that E was a better name, and so he changed it, then, and there, in the registry in Manchester. At least, this is how the story is told. The name change was not a popular decision, and my mother was left to suffer with two names for the rest of her life. It was K to friends, always, but E to every official document she signed and mail she received. From the standpoint of her children, K's life has been defined by the choices she has made that placed her children's interests before her own. Perhaps fittingly, she has spent the majority of her working life in the child protection agency, though that, she says, has its limits. It is getting time to retire. She'll do it slowly. One of her friends asked if she would like to go to Alice Springs and work for one of the outreach programs there. She laughed. 'My retirement plan is not to do the same job with less pay and worse hours,' she told him.

N

No, A Dialogue –

No.

                              No?

Fucking insulting of you to say so.

                     Don't fucking raise your voice!

                        People can hear.

I don't fucking care.

Let them think fucking white trash. I don't give a shit what strangers think of me.

                              Well—

No.

No excuses.

If I didn't wanna be here, I wouldn't.

I didn't have to fucking come to Brisbane. *You* got the job behind the
mic up here, not me.I could've stayed the fuck down in Sydney,
worked my classes, run some extras, written what I wanted,
and got by, as you just said.

I could've done that. I would've had friends down there.
You're the only friend I got up here—everyone else is
just some kind of acquaintance. But I didn't stay.

I came up here.

I came up here for you, not this fucking heat.

                                                    I know that!

Then why are you being a *cunt*?

Well?

                                          I can't believe you said that.

As opposed to all the other things you've implied so far? That I'm a
fucking loser? That I don't want to get a job?

Call *A Current Affair* and sick Ray Martin on me!

                                             I never said that.

Yeah, but you been implying it since

I got home.

                                                        ...

Fuck it.

I'm fucking done eating, are you?

Nationality – When I say that I am Australian, I do not really know what that means. To an extent, I know that it means that I was born in Australia. But it is just a location. I might as well say that I am British. That I am Pakistani. I could have been born in any one of those locations, had my parents decided to travel around the time of my birth. Perhaps I would feel less confusion over what it means to be Australian if I had been born in a plane, over international waters, completely independent from any nation for birth. The International Water's Baby. But I am not such. I am Australian. I am told it is important, but not why. It does not explain my skin colour, my agnosticism, my lack of patriotism, nor my decision to write. I don't know what it explains. I do know, however, that when I am sitting next to Z, who is Chinese, and she is explaining to me how a Chinese boy she has seen might be a bit too FOB (Fresh Off the Boat) for her tastes, that I cannot use the term like she does. Even if I were to say it in the gently ironic way that she has, my whiteness would instantly translate it into something dark and unpleasant.

Nationalism – Nationalism leaves me cold. I find people who are filled with a national pride, no matter where they're from, irritating. It could be that I am like this because I do not have their pride, and so it is my lack resisting their have, though I do not feel as if I lack something. It is true that I am not proud of Australia, but this does not mean that I hate the country, the people, or the customs; nor do I think it has been a bad country to live in. It isn't. It is quite a lovely country, and I like living here. I haven't lived anywhere else and I have no desire to do so. But Australia is not perfect. It has very real problems to go with its beauty. In that, it is like other countries, and that makes it no better than America. No better than Israel. No better than Iran. When I hear people argue freedoms and beliefs and tell me that one country is better than another, it just angers me. Nationalism equals ownership: of country, of culture, of past, and of future. It ignores that fact that a country is just part of the planet, that the planet is part of the solar system, that the solar system part of that universe. You don't get born with a right of ownership for any of that.

National Pride Experiment – Buy thirty-two different flags and a big, two litre plastic tub of bleach. In a safe place, bleach each flag until there is not one trace of colour to be seen, but the designs still remain. Then ask people what the most important thing about a flag is.

Native – On the 26th of January, 1788, the continent that would be renamed Australia, was invaded. In Parramatta, the second settlement of the British, there is a mural across the long, looping path that runs alongside Parramatta River depicting this. It begins in blue. Soon, three ships appear. It is eight ships short. From these ships disembark British soldiers in red uniforms. There are no convicts. No mention of the five hundred and forty eight men and one hundred and eighty eight women who have been thrown from their homes. There is also no mention of the one hundred and sixty thousand men, women, and children who will be sent in shackles. Who will sit in dank, fetid holes for the long voyage. Some will not make it. On the now sand colour mural, the red uniformed British are lifting their rifles. They fire. At the front, two have spears in them. Soon, Aboriginal men lie dead on the ground. Blood from bullets holes. There is no hint of the disease. No hint that the British will separate their families. In fact, these pitch-black men look angry. It looks like they are attacking the British. History records that the first meetings between the natives and invaders were not violent. That many of Aboriginal people believed the British to be the ghosts of ancestors, returning. But the very red British soldiers on the mural are clearly responding to the pitch-black attackers. You pass a tent next. You see a hand. A white hand. A British hand. It does not have any shackles. It is holding a brown hand. Not a black hand. The colouring is different, lighter, obviously lighter. It hints at the diluted state of Aboriginal heritage, but does not explain how this has come about. People of two colours are standing together beneath the hands. They stand together on the cement path of Parramatta, which was first called Burramatta, but changed because a British man could not pronounce the word. The hands clutch each other tightly, surrounded by the clean, simple, white history that many promote. Surrounded by lies.

Naturalism – Mum has been working at Burnside Home. The Catholic Church runs it, but, with the rise of Capitalist Thought, which argues that everything must turn a profit, even a charity for the homeless, they have been cutting back facilities and selling off land. One day, Mum tells it, they'll cut back her job. She is fifty-three. Fortunately, the Australian Government begins a new child protection agency and she applies and eventually, gets a job. But to have the job, she must give up her British Citizenship. She has to be naturalised. She laughs when they tell her this, and says, sure. Her parents, well in their eighties, think it is a good idea, because then the Government can't send her back home. They fear being deported, even still. She tells them that the job pays almost twice of what she was getting at Burnside and that is why she will do it. On the night of her citizenship ceremony, she is given a Bottle Brush, a tree with reddish, brush like flowers that is native to Australia. She gives it to her father, because she thinks the tree is ugly.

Nation – If Capitalist Thought is a problem within a charity organisation, then it is more of a problem in the running of a country. A country is not a company, but each Government who wins a term in office treats it as such, thinking only to the end of their term. Over the years, the Australian Government and State Governments have sold off a nation wide bank, airports in various States, roads in every part of the country, and other pieces of land and public owned businesses that they have been able to slice up, little by little, until they own nothing. When they make political alliances, they talk of the business it will bring. They think of the budget. The bottom line. They tell people that if they don't vote for them, then their home loan rates will rise. But a country is not a business. There are more important concerns than if a good oil line can be secured if you help drive out rebels in your neighbouring country.

New Australia – In 1893, the Australian movement called The New Australia Co-Operative Settlement Association officially founded a socialist colony in Paraguay. It was called the *Colonia Nueva Australia*. Led by William Lane, the New Australia Movement, as they were known, told people that they could come and work as free men, labour on land owned by all for the good of all, and not be bothered by selfish, singular needs. However, problems developed immediately over the prohibition of alcohol, relations with the locals, and Lane's leadership. It was, without the socialist rhetoric, rather much like the old Australia, which still had problems with the locals, and had once had leadership problems that resulted in the country being run on a currency of rum that British soldiers supplied and traded for land ownership with free men. In the New Australia, one year after its founding, Lane and group of his followers left to begin a new socialist utopia, and the Paraguayan Government was left to distribute the land to individual owners.

Nabokov, Vladimir – In my copy of Vladimir Nabokov's *Pale Fire*, I keep the hand written letter that my Nanna sent, and which details her recipe for pastry, in particular pie. When I was a child, her apple pie was the thing I loved the most. It is an old British recipe, reportedly taken from the nineteenth century when her mother, who worked in a bakery, used it. Here it is, transcribed in full:

> *First: Cook Fruit –*
> If making a pie, cook fruit first. Here is example of how to ready apples for pie: get 4 granny smith apples. Peel and core. Slice apples, place in saucepan, run cold water over apples, then pour water off, leaving about two tablespoons of water. Add about two tablespoons sugar, cook until soft, let cool. Once done, mash with fork and place in dish. This will stop apples from turning brown.
> *Second: Pastry –*
> 8 oz, self rising flour.
> 1 tablespoon cornflower.
> Pinch of salt (if sweet pastry, 1 dessertspoon of sugar).

4½ oz butter (or 2½ oz butter &
2 oz lard for traditional way).
2 oz cold water (just enough to hold it together).
Mixing:
Sift flour twice into bowl. Add chopped fat and mix into flour
with chopper. Then add gradually just enough water to form a
ball by squeezing together gently with your hand. Cut into
Half.
Then:
Flour the board and roll out pastry to size of plate. Put in
fruit. Moisten lightly round edges of plate before placing top
pastry on. Use handle of dessert spoon and pinch edges. Use a
form and prick top of pastry all over. Sprinkle a little sugar on
the top of the pie. Put into hot oven at about 190 degrees.
Cook for 25 minutes.
Note: Do not use tinned pie fruit!

Nation –

O

Orwell, George – Born Eric Blair, but renamed for literature, the great author, George Orwell, died at the age of forty-six from tuberculosis. It has been suggested that he contracted the beginnings of the disease during the period of his life that he spent living in poverty. Following this logic, one can, if one wishes, portray Orwell's death as one that has occurred in the pursuit of authenticity, as that period of his life resulted in the writing of *Down and Out in Paris and London*. However, the author's years of poverty and his recollections of the time are not exactly true (though they are not outright lies, either, his biographers are quick to assure). In one biography, *Orwell: the Life*, D. J. Taylor recounts how, in a copy of *Down and Out in Paris and London* that Orwell presented to a friend, the author wrote in the margin notes on the authenticity of his experience. The third chapter, detailing how one can survive in poverty, reads, "Succeeding chapters not actually autobiography, but drawn from what I have seen."

Outcast – I am nineteen and I attend the launch of a new bookstore. It is there that I meet my first authors. They are in their forties, their fifties, and they are all male, all white, and all grey haired. Some are overweight, some are slim. One has a moustache. They are browns and greys and blues, collectively. The owner of the bookstore, who I have met a few weeks before, introduces me, and the authors begin advising me on how to cheat on my tax returns. Everything is deductible, a tall author says. Having never filed a tax return, I can only respond by nodding. Shortly after, they begin talking about television and movies and I sit and I listen. Not one of them talks about books.

Organisations Are Compromise – The Cubs wanted me to work for badges. The soccer team wanted me to be the goal keeper. The Red Cross wanted me to door knock. The Christian Group said I had to read the Bible. The school council wanted me to participate. The office job wanted me to wear a tie, plus shoes. Not sneakers. Definitely not sneakers. Shave, also. The projectionist job wanted me to stop reading between films. The Greens Party wanted me to stand on a street and sell a newspaper. Writing Groups wanted me to be polite. Scientologists wanted my money. The Anti-War Group wanted me to wear a t-shirt. A teaching job wanted me to wear less black. Unless it was a lifestyle choice, she added, hurriedly. I can not remember when it was that an organisation last asked me what I wanted.

Observatory – A friend of my father's worked in Siding Springs Observatory and when I was young, both of them would take their children to look through the telescopes at night. The first time is one of earliest memories. I remember walking through snow, wrapped up in a jumper, a parker, a scarf, a beanie, and wearing orange gum boots. The observatory itself is a collection of snow white domes located on the top of a mountain some forty minutes outside the town Coonabarabran, which is located in the dry outback of NSW. But at night, in winter, they sit on the mountain like pale, fallen moons that have fallen from the sky. They are lodged, now, in my memory, in the mountain's rock, and surrounded by snow. With my non-family Uncle in the lead, and Dad bringing up the rear, us four children walk past the domes and enter. Inside, we have to be lifted to the telescope eyepiece, but through it, we can make out the swirling mass of colours that make up the planets around us.

Oxygen – We learn to speak from the dead words in the dead air around us. Meanings are taught to us through experience, through use. Phrases we learn from our parents. Our teachers. Our friends.

Our enemies. It is a certain truth to say that we have learnt to speak by regurgitating sounds that we have heard. We are all mimics. We apply meaning to them, but that meaning is arbitrary, is slippery, is malleable and changeable. The words of adoration we speak are not our own. Our hate is learned. Our expressions of joy. Language spoken from our mouths is not alive. It is dead. Caught in the dead air, recycled, reused, to the point that the personal origin is lost to repetition.

Obscenities I Like To Use – *Fuck.* Used politely, used angrily, used as adverb and a verb. It has a lot of mobility in it, as a word. I barely notice when people use it. *Shit.* Not so much. When something goes bad. After the toilet. To describe something that is not very good. *Cock.* When talking dirty. When describing a male I don't like. Occasionally, I add sucker to it. Cocksucker. *Cock*sucker, I say. Gets a laugh. *Wank.* For when something is self indulgent. *Wanker*, for a person. *Fucker*, the same. *Asshole.* Insult. *Cunt.* Always cunt. Talking dirty. Insults. Endearment. Love.

Oral Stimulation. A Dialogue –

Hey!

...

Hey!

...Yeah?

I didn't like that.

No.

No, neither did I.

So.

91

Yeah.

I'm—I'm sorry.

Yeah?

Yeah.

...

Yeah.

I'm sorry too.

It was shitty, I shouldn't have said those things. I shouldn't have called you a cunt. I don't use the word like that. It's not right.

It's just—I'm just frustrated, that's all.

I know. So am I.

Ah...

...Fuck it.

Come here.

What?

Shh.

...

...What was that for?

Fuck fighting.

I want to be fucked in the ass tonight.

You've been promising me I could fuck you in the ass all day.

I've been all wet for it.

I saw the photos.

I saw your cock, too. What do you do, go to the toilet to photo it?

That's why we got the phones with cameras.

You can take films, too.

I want to be filmed.

Filming you makes me want to fuck you.

I want to get home and fuck. I want to feel your cum inside me.

I'll make the baby eat the cum.

Objectionable – I have never understood censorship. It often seems to me that to keep the moral standards, whatever they may be, people are made to live lives that have been dramatically compartmentalised. All mention of homosexuality is stripped out of *A Street Car Named Desire*, but Tennessee Williams' play, from which the film was made, remains, while performances of the play continue still. Yet it was important, at the time the film was being made, that no homosexuality be referenced. The film could not have been made if it did. An erect penis is an X-rated commodity, yet a large portion of the population comes into contact with one (and sometimes more) daily. Swear words are banned from the radio, but a little patch of silence exists, and the listener can speak it in its absence. On the television, you can see the lips move. Harry Potter is banned for promoting witchcraft, but a entire genre exists that does the same. Blood is removed from swords in films, but on the News, children lie in hospital beds with missing limbs, and bloody bandages. If there is anything that is truly obscene in this life, it is the sheer idiocy and righteousness that censorship presents itself; and worse, that people believe it is in our best interests.

Orwell, George – P is a beautiful woman. Physically, she is one of the most beautiful women I have met; in addition, she is intelligent, articulate, and passionate. It is true, however, that beauty is a subjective experience, and so what one will find beautiful, another may not. I will therefor resist describing her. Imagine her as you must. The problem with P was that she thought I was brilliant, and told me so, repeatedly. What made my brilliance more amazing to her, was that I had risen out of a poor, working class environment. Being poor, she told me, made my art more credible. More authentic. On the day that she says that, I tell her that I didn't grow up poor, and that being poor doesn't make you more real. When you're poor, you just have less choices. I had more choices than some, I add, but she ignores that. Instead, she tells me that George Orwell wrote the same thing in *Down and Out in Paris and London*. It occurs to me that while she is beautiful and I want her, she is a day tripper, a girl visiting my life for the experience of it, and I will not be used like that.

P

Phobia – Push bikes. Gone by six. Mum would walk behind me, waiting to catch. Dad's solution was to take the training wheels off. Heights. Gone by eight. No reason. Water. Swimming pools only. Ocean and bath tubs fine. Gone by fourteen. Made worse by the time when I was five and Dad threw me into a pool to learn how to swim. Made even worse when a friend's mother tried to drown me at nine. Soccer balls to the face. Solved by no longer playing soccer. Motorbikes. Phobia arrived at ten, when I crashed a motorbike and burnt the inside of my right leg on the muffler quite horribly. Scar still there. At nineteen took lessons to get over phobia. Ladders. Still existing. Escalators. Still existing. Herds of undomesticated wildlife. They watch me. Murders of magpies and crows at top of list. Parachuting. Actually, stepping out of planes with or without parachute. Still existing. Closed in spaces. Moderate. Cars. Growing. I dream of cars. I dream of them all, if they are still phobias. I have been dreaming since 1976.

Pamphlet – In 2000, I created the Urban Sprawl Project. It was a small, black and white pamphlet that mixed photography and prose, the writing of which was focused on Sydney. It was a work of psychogeography, not concerned with creating an accurate portrayal of the area that I was writing about. Instead, it sought to overwrite it, to distort it, to create a new way of looking at the environment around me. From the start, I knew there was no audience for it, so I decided that I would distribute it for free, putting the finished product into the letter boxes of people who lived in the area. C liked the idea and he offered to cover the costs of printing it, full well knowing that he would never make it back. So on our off days, we walked around suburbs with a bag full of cheap, disposable cameras, and photographed anything that interested us. We would spend about a week walking through every corner of the suburbs we wrote about. We photographed every bit of urban decay, every bit of new urban site, and every person that we could. C's photos were nearly always useless: shots of sky, shots of fingers, shots of security cameras, and hundreds of shots of blurry security guards, approaching the pair of us.

Perry, Anne – Novelist Anne Perry was born Juliet Hulme. She, along with her friend Pauline Parker, were responsible for the murder of Parker's mother in Christchurch, New Zealand, when they were sixteen. The defining characteristic of this murder was that Park, with a brick in a stocking, was forced to strike her mother forty-five times in the head to murder her. Hulme's part in the event was at an organisational level; she also began the event by dropping an ornament, which Parker's mother to bent down to pick up and thus exposed herself to the attack of her daughter. The two girls killed her because they feared that Parker's mother was going to break up their friendship, which she objected to on the grounds that she through the two were too close. After serving five years in a women's prison, both girls were released, under the proviso that they not contact each other. Since them, Hulme, under the name of Anne Perry, has made a successful career out of writing historical murder mysteries and, since 1979, has published over 50 books. The literary world, unconcerned by her chosen genre and its link to her past, have remained silent over the fact. Perhaps they believe that it provides her with an authenticity that other mystery writers lack.

Primary School – I went to Toongabbie Primary School. In year one, I met J. He maintains that we met in year two. We were in the same class in year two, but I maintain year one. We both met D in year three. He maintains that on the first day in the school, a girl lifted her skirt for him, and showed off her bloomers. There, his story begins. Before I went to school, the teachers in the pre-school my parents sent me to warned by mother and father that I was so painfully shy that I would find it very difficult to fit in and that I would make no friends.

Pacifier – In 2002, the New Zealand born, but most Australian based band, Shihad, changed their name to Pacifier. Originally named after members of the band misheard the word jihad in a David Lynch film, they were now concerned, in the aftermath of September 11th, that their mishearing would be reproduced on a global level, and result in backlash. The name change was not greeted with approval by fans, and the one Pacifier album released was considered to be a dull affair. Pacifier received a lot of attention, however, arguably more than Shihad. In 2005, however, after touring as Pacifier, the band returned to the name Shihad and released *Love is the New Hate*, their most political album to date. It was inspired by their experiences as Pacifier and touring through the United States. This album was greeted with unanimous approval as was the return to the band name.

Photographer – While I enjoy photography, I am under no false impressions about my ability. I am strictly a cheap and dirty street photographer. The quicker I can take a picture, the better. I am interested in moments when people are lost in their thoughts. When their guard is down. When everything in life just meets perfectly for an instant. But for a while, I entertained the idea that I might make a good photographer. Then I met Q, who works as a photographer and fashion designer. Sitting in her apartment one night, looking through her portfolio, and looking at the large photographs across the walls, I could see the limitations of my ability, the ceiling I could never hope to pass. I do not have the raw ability, the dedication, or the love, to become not just good, not just passable, but something special. I would not give up things that are important to me to push myself further. I could not make photography an art.

Psalmanazar, George – At the age of 25, and in the year 1704, George Psalmanazar authored a book entitled *A Historical and Geographical Description of Formosa, an Island Subject to the Emperor of Japan*. Claiming to be a native born man from the city, he wrote about how Formosa had such a wealthy economy that men walked around naked, except for the gold and silver plates they kept over their genitals for modesty's sake. In addition, the society was polygamous, and men could take as many wives as they pleased. Psalmanazar also insisted that the natives ate serpents, executed murderers by shooting their bodies with arrows while they hanged upside down, and annually sacrificed the hearts of eighteen thousand young boys to the gods. Priests would later eat the bodies in a showing of waste not want not. Two years later, he revealed his hoax after public criticisms. It was not a very believable hoax, even three hundred years ago, it appears. The strangeness, however, occurs later in his life, when Psalmanazar became incredibly religious. During this time, he began to write articles about the real conditions of Formosa, purposefully criticising his earlier lies and the people who had believed them.

Plausible – One of the hardest things to teach in fiction is plausibility. Ultimately, you cannot teach it full: it either works because the reader is willing to believe you, or it doesn't, for much the same reason. For some, it will never work. There is a large body of people out there who do not read fiction because it is not plausible. Instead, they read histories, biographies, and other non-fiction books that while they are not as true as they often claim to be, overcome the disbelief barrier because they are presented as truth. The ability to be able to create fake plausibility remains, however, one of the most important things for an author of fiction. Without it, he or she will not succeed in creating a body of paying work: readers buy when they believe an author. Readers buy because of truth. Truth is the commodity of literature.

Pornography –

Personal Diary Entry, October 12th – *Six months since my last entry. So much has changed.*

Q

Query – I was not taught that there was good and evil. When I had a question about what was right, and what was wrong, I was told about personal responsibility.

Questionable Morality Story, the Introduction – The old school photos tell me that I met N on the first day of school. My memory does not know, but she was in the same class, so I must have. The old school photos show her as white, brown haired, and with pigtails, but that's not my memory of her. She is older, still brown haired, but now shaped and curved, and with a soft, feminine voice, and nasty sense of humour. In the final years of High School, I had a huge crush on her. It took me, roughly, a year to work up to the point where I was confident that if I asked her out, she would say yes. Before I did that, however, I made the mistake of listening to W, a close friend of mine. As the story must present at this part, he wanted her as well, and because there must always be a loser, I kept my mouth shut, and waited, hoping that she would say no. She didn't, of course. We have all seen the movies. We know how it goes. After High School, and despite meeting other girls (who I had more in common), I was unable to get over N. At twenty, I decided that the only responsible and forthright thing to do was to break up her relationship with W and steal her away. I was his best friend, sure, but you know the cliché about friends and a girl.

101

Quixote – I do not vote. I have a t-shirt that says DON'T VOTE and I wear it at election time. In Australia, not voting is illegal, but I do it anyway, because I believe that democracy is about being able to make a choice. That also includes the choice *not* to vote. When people find out that I don't vote, the first thing they say is, 'You should! There are people in other countries dying for the right!' They then say, 'Now you have no right to complain about the country.' I laugh at the latter, and then explain that while I do believe that everyone should have the right to decide their Government, I live in a country where everyone can vote; indeed, they *must* vote; and my country still has problems. My needs are different to those of someone who cannot vote. Democracy, it seems to me, is too often confused as the solution to the World's political problems.

Quotidian – Governments lie to us all the time, and we accept that, knowingly.

Questionable Morality Story, the Main Part – N was calling me. She was emailing me. She was inviting me out to lunch. W didn't know about it. Occasionally, she would tell me that she was thinking of leaving W, who I was no longer friends with. He didn't have any friends now, she said, and that made it difficult to leave. I shrugged when she told me. Then, one day, I picked up the phone. It was W. He was crying. He wanted to talk. Wanted to talk to me. *Please*. Unable to say no (and thinking that I had won and N had broken up with him, and that I would be benevolent in this moment) I agreed to meet him. There, still crying, still sobbing, he told me that he had cancer. *Cancer?* What the fuck? No, no, this was *not* what was meant to be happening. *No.* But still, there was W, blond haired, crying, looking for friend, for sympathy, for understanding. Soon, he began telling me that he would never be able to marry N. That all he wanted to do was marry N. That he loved her more than anything in the world. In a short amount of time, I felt like complete and utter shit. I could feel my want for N dissolve the more he talked. Could feel it drain out of me, in way that a cyst is drained. In a confused daze, I listened, unsure what else to do. What could I say? I had no idea, but when W

102

rose, and began to leave, he paused, and asked if we could go back to being friends. I ran my hand over my head. Sighed. Then said, 'I'm not going to be your friend just cause you got cancer.'

Quit – Will I become tired of complaining about the lies that our Government tells? They wear me down and the anger is hard to keep.

Quisling – If there is no good or evil, then why am I so caught up in the fact that the Government is lying? Am I traitor to my own ideals? The morals of right wing politicians are not mine, thank you, but does that make them wrong? Does it make me? If neither of us are right, and neither of us are wrong, then why do I argue against their decisions regarding stem cells, the banning of abortion, and the War on Terror, to name just a few? I cannot even argue that the majority of people want the things that I believe in place. So why am I unquestioning in my belief that I am right, and they are wrong?

Questionable Morality Story, the Conclusion – I never heard from W after that. N, for a bit, but the pursuit was too difficult, too complex, and my interest had gone. Would it come back? Who knew. One day, she stopped contacting me. Later, I heard that she and W had gotten engaged. They are married now. Occasionally, I run into them: awkward, strained moments. I always take the time, however, to note that W appears to be in good health. That he shows absolutely no signs of being treated for cancer. That no one ever speaks about him having cancer. That, in fact, I appear to be the only one who knows anything about his "cancer". One day, I will have to ask him about it.

Queensland. Personal Diary, October 12th – *When I came back to Sydney I could feel its absence.*

Quota – Sometimes, you just got to say, 'Fuck it.'

R

Racism – I do not tolerate racism. In a group of people, I am that person who corrects the other. There is no reason that I will accept for it. I react the same way to those who discriminate against homosexuals.

Religion – I never went to Church regularly. Once, after staying the night at J's, his mum made us go to a Sunday morning mass. It was a strange event that was never repeated again. Other than that, I have only been to Church for funerals, weddings, and births. I have also been into churches unofficially. Mostly, I have been to take photos, because despite myself, I find myself quite attracted to the way the big, stain glassed churches look. They are beautiful. Churches and mosques are perhaps the only beautiful thing about organised religion. Most of my religious contact, then, has come from literature, news, and individuals. Even in a public High School, they made sure we had a little bit of religious education, and so they made us go to Scripture once a term. It never took me long before I was getting into trouble. A Scripture teacher—usually a volunteer from the local churches—once told me that sacrificing yourself for another was the most giving and important thing you could do. I asked him if he had ever heard of Survivor Sickness. When he said no, I explained to him that Survivor Sickness was what happened to those who survived disasters. They feel, I told him, that they are left with the awful weight of responsibility to make their life meaningful, to give it

105

purpose, for they believe that their lives must be worth something now that others have perished beside it. The Scripture teacher told me that I obviously didn't know what I was talking about.

Racism – Growing up, Mum used to talk a lot about *those* people. *Those* people trying to come into the country illegally. *Those* people marrying for visas. *Those* people bringing their families over after them. The contradiction of being a migrant herself who had been in a family who had done the last did not occur to her. We would argue in the car. We would argue at home. We never argued about homework. Never argued about the times I should be home. Never about what I should do with my life. No, we only argued about *those* people. After fifteen years of arguing, Mum rarely says it now, though I suspect she has just learnt not to say it around me. She votes for the Conservative Government, still, and they traded on the threat of *those* people in last two elections quite profitably.

Religion – As I have mentioned, the only bands that I knew and saw when I was growing up were Christian Rock Bands. Too young for gigs in pubs, too poor for the pop bands that our parents would let us go too, C and I spent at least one Friday night a month in the early nineties going to Christian Rock Gigs. Neither of us were religious, but the gig was never more than five bucks and if you ignored the lyrics and the sermon in the middle, it wasn't so bad. For most of the sermons, C and I would disappear outside, taking the girls we had just met; but we stayed every now and then for the laugh. Once, we listened to a guy with tattoos, ripped jeans and a bandana on his head talk about how he had become Born Again. As it always is with Born Again Rockers, the singer had been living a life of meaningless sex and drugs. This one was also involved in mugging people on the street. In his sermon, he likened the finding of God to the time a business man had punched him in the mouth, busting up his teeth. He pulled out his false teeth to show us the truth. He held them high and proud and stained yellow from cigarettes. What made the punch (and God) so dramatic was that he didn't see it coming, he said. It just happened. *Boom.* Fast forward an hour, and C and I are walking home when two guys, a little drunk and a little stoned, come up to us. They want cigarettes. They want money. One of them takes the hat I am wearing. I grab him. I figure I know where this is going so I hit him. Square in the mouth. Once. Twice. I am thinking about God. I am going for the third time when C stops me. The guy I hit is spitting out his teeth on the ground. I thank God.

Racism – The year eight class I was in had a reputation. One of those bad reputations. It was in this class that I met C. By the end of the first term, the class had gone through one Math teacher and two Science teachers. In the final weeks, the class was busy breaking down a third Science teacher, an Indian woman who had just finished her degree. I cannot remember her name, but one of my classmates had named her Ms Kalabalablacksnake. It was his idea, also, to bring in the golliwog biscuits. You can't buy them anymore, but they were, basically, chocolate flavoured biscuits shaped like golliwogs, which were based off a children's book by Florence Upton. On the day that golliwogs came to the classroom, I knew about the racial content of the golliwog, as did the rest of the call—all thirty of us, a mix of backgrounds that were white, Indian, Asian, Greek, and Kiwi. Yet, despite all our racial differences, despite knowing the racism in the biscuit, each one of us sat with the fucking biscuit in our fucking hands and we all sang, when the Indian teacher entered, 'Golliwog me, golliwog you, we all want to be a golliwog too' at the top of our lungs. She burst into tears and quit, right there. It is not my proudest moment.

Religion – Two American Mormons knock on my door. One is white, the other black. They are both wearing white shirts, neatly pressed, and black pants, also pressed. Each has a black name badge. They are Missionaries. I see them all the time in Sydney, always in pairs. Generally, if approached, I just say no, not interested, and that is it. But some are pushy. The white one in this pair is pushy. He wants to save my soul. He wants to know why I don't want to save my soul. I like my soul the way it is, but he is righteous. Finally, I say, 'Okay, I tell you what, I'll make a bet. I'll tell you guys one joke. After the joke, you can decide if I need to learn about your Jesus. If so, I'll listen. If not, you got to go away, and leave me be. Sound good?' The black Mormon smiles, but the earnest white Mormon nods, and agrees. I figure a lot of religious types are secret gamblers. So I smile, step back, give myself plenty of room, and then I say, 'How does Jesus chew his nails?' The black Mormon says nothing, but his smile grows. The white one shakes his head. I pause a little longer. I hold it. I look into the eyes of the white Mormon. They're blue. Cold. Seriously. I continue to smile. And then. And then suddenly. And then suddenly I begin making chewing noises on the palms of my hands. Loud chewing noises. Feasting noises. Hannibal Lector at a buffet feasting noises. I slobber. I gnaw. After a while, I lower my hand. The black Mormon is trying not to laugh. The white Mormon doesn't need to try. He lifts up his Bible. He points it at me. Then he says, 'Sir, we are Mormons. We are here to spread the word about our Lord and Saviour, Jesus Christ. The Lord and Saviour you have just mocked. And if you want to know about him, you will have to come and find us.' And then they left.

Racism – I am white, but because I am white, the fact is not important. When people talk about my life, or they critique my writing, they do not write about me as a white person. It is possible that they will write about me as an Australian, especially if they are from America, where my country of birth is given a friendly, holiday exoticism; but they will not write about me as a white Australian, just as in Australia people will not write about a white American. The colour of my skin is not seen, and so other attributes of me are. I will be written about as a male, but I will not be written about as a heterosexual male. I can be written about as working class. As a protestor. As under educated, over educated, and just plain educated. I will even be written about as a big, mean, bald guy dressed in black. But throughout this all, the colour of my skin is invisible, and the colour of everyone who is not white, noticeable.

Religion – At the beginning of the last semester at the coaching college, no students show up to one of my year nine classes. It happens. Sometimes they are on holidays. Sometimes they have convinced their parents to not send them to school on Sunday. I understand. It is an hour and a half before my next class, so I end up talking to the boss. We talk about Israel. They have just begun bombing Lebanon. We agree that Israel has escalated the violence unnecessarily. Then he tells me that it is to be expected. The Jews killed Jesus, after all. For a moment, I do not know how to react. Then he tells me that Jews control the World's Media. This is why news reportage is pro-Israeli. I choke back a laugh. Finally, he tells me that Judaism tells Jews that they will rule the World. Finally, I manage to say that most religions tell the believers that, in one form or another, and he stares at me, before he repeats that the Jews killed Jesus. I try not to laugh at him again.

Racism – I write from a white male's point of view. It is the only way that I can write. I cannot speak for another culture, another experience, another gender, and I do not. This, however, does not mean that I will not write about homosexual Sri Lankan-American girls, Japanese teachers, Aboriginal cops, bisexual white Australian country girls, homosexual Greek-Australian men, and whatever other set of attributes that I decide upon. If I write only of white, heterosexual males, then I will be writing the same character, again and again. It will be that I am writing to the truth that I have, but I will not be pushing myself as an author. I will be playing it safe. But more than that, I will not be accurately portraying the environment that I live in. Mine is the multicultural world, the mongrel world, the mash and crash of cultures, ideals, and skin colour. I will portray this world in my work.

Religion – The one thing I will tolerate, openly, is people who are intolerant of organised religion. Is that contradiction too much?

S

Stripper – I am walking on the long, empty road that leads out from the University of Western Sydney with H, who works as a stripper. We are walking to a train station. She says, 'Would you ever date a stripper?'

Sex –

Sanctity – Don't talk about fucking. Don't fuck until you're in love. Don't fuck someone too old. Don't fuck someone too young. Don't fuck in the ass. Don't fuck in the mouth. Don't fuck in groups. Don't freeze your cum after fucking. Don't drink your fucking frozen cum after fucking. Don't fuck in public. Don't fuck strangers. Don't take drugs while fucking. Don't get drunk cause you might fuck someone you shouldn't fuck. Don't fuck in costumes. Don't fuck dead bodies. Don't fuck animals. Don't fuck to porn. Don't fucking make porn. Don't watch your friends fuck. Don't fucking put things up your ass for the entire fucking day. Don't buy fuck dolls. Don't buy fuck dolls that look like your dead partner. Don't pay for fucking. Don't fucking cheat. If you cheat, change the fucking sheets. Don't fuck with food. Don't use food in fucking. Don't fuck as famous as people. Don't fuck famous people. Don't fuck in the bathtub. You're sitting in your own fucking filth. Fuck in the shower. Don't make her fucking call you daddy. Don't make him fucking call you mummy. Don't fuck your parents. Don't fuck your children. Don't fuck your cousins unless twice removed. Or in Texas. Don't fuck without protection. Don't fuck on the first date. Don't keep a fucking list of people you fucked. Don't add to the list while the last fuck is there. Don't ask if you were a good fuck. Don't ask how your fucking compares to others. Don't fuck for revenge. Don't fuck to pass the time. Don't fuck to fuck. Fuck that. Fuck sanctity. Fucking ruins everything.

Stranger – *Naked Came the Stranger* was published in 1969 under the name Penelope Ashe. It was, however, conceived originally by Mike McGrady, who believed that the American literary culture had become so empty that a work with no literary merits would succeed if it had enough sex in it. To prove his theory he, and a group of males who believed the same, wrote *Naked Came the Stranger,* a deliberately bad novel, filled with inconsistencies and mediocre writing, and which detailed the experience of an unfaithful wife. The book was published and, yes, was a success at the time. Due to its success, however, some of the contributors felt that they should reveal the truth, and did so. They revealed themselves on national television. Reportedly, this put the book on the New York Times Best Seller list, and sold more copies than it had when it was about sex.

Sexuality – Bisexuality is the sexuality that slips through the cracks. It is seen by many as being an experimental phase, a moment of curiosity that young men and women explore, before (so says the misguided common thought) they discover that there is nothing enjoyable in having sex with partners of the same gender, and return to monogamous heterosexuality. Indeed, while in a relationship, a bisexual individual will often be called heterosexual or homosexual, as if the one or the other is truly the only options of sexuality out there.

STD – V has genital herpes. She tells me with caution, with reluctance, but she tells me. It is an after effect, the stain of an event in her life that she cannot forget. The disease makes her dirty, she tells me. She is no longer pure. Her loss of innocence, loss of trust, loss of so much, is tied into the herpes that she cannot cure. It is the physical manifestation of her pain. I listen. I am glad she tells me. I tell her that it doesn't bother me. That there are protections. But the burden is too much, and she will not have sex. She says that she cannot.

Simulation – Britney Spears was taught how to simulate sensuality, without actually having an intimate knowledge of sex. This is, of course, if you believe the press releases at the time. Later, it was revealed that she did know the intimacies. But the truth is not as interesting, in this case, as the idea that society found it more morally acceptable to have an ignorant teenage girl turned into an object of sexual desire. For the audience, Spears was about sex. It was not the music that drew people in, but rather her youth, and the provocative poses that her music directors, art directors, and mother, allowed her to be portrayed in. For a brief moment, Britney Spears, underage, illegal, was sex. But because the girl herself was portrayed as ignorant, innocent, and forever virginal, there was no problem in this, it seems.

Sixty Plus – D decides to take a holiday in Port Macquarie. It is five hours drive out of Sydney, and he tells me I should come and split the driving with him. His grandparents are away, so we will be able to stay in their house. Port, as the locals call it, is the popular destination of retirees. Upon our arrival we see elderly men and women everywhere. Anyone who is not elderly is in the employment for them, running the cinemas, the diners, and the jet skis down by the ocean. Early on, D and I go looking for a map. While I ask about maps, D ends up in the back of the news agency and comes across a magazine called *Sixty Plus*. He buys it to show me. On the cover are two grey haired women, mostly undressed, and in a more than friendly embrace. Despite myself, I look inside. It is my first exposure to retiree porn.

Sexism – I was called a misogynist, once. It sticks in me still.

Sleazy – D likes to tell J and I about his sex. He tells us when he gets drunk. He tells us when he is high. He tells us mostly when he is sober, however. We have names for the stories. The Blob of Flesh, in which he woke up next to a girl who was the Blob of Flesh. ('I lifted the blanket and there she was, man, like a blob of flesh.') There was the Starfish, an old high school girlfriend he seduced on the rebound when she was living in his place. ('She was like a starfish. Just lay there, you know, all open.) And there was the Porn Girl, who he actually likes to call the Editor Girl because she was an editor at a large publishing company, but who I renamed after having to listen to him one night with J. ('She had all this eye contact, man. Like a fucking film.') He asks ex-girlfriends if his penis is big enough for them. After they break up, he insists. They won't lie then.

Sixteen – A is sixteen. She sends me a pictures of her naked. In some, she is masturbating. In others, she is in the shower. Sometimes she is wearing her school uniform. She tells me she wants to fuck. She describes in detail how she wants to fuck me. I tell her how I will.

Sex –

T

Truth – In his war memoirs, the German born, Nobel Prize winning author, Günter Grass, revealed that at the end of World War II, he served in a tank unit in the Waffen SS. He was seventeen at the time. The Waffen SS units are infamously known for being the guards of the concentration camps in which so much horror happened, and are also reported to have been responsible for other war crimes during the war. While Grass himself has never denied that he served in the army after his conscription (rather like Pope Benedict XVI), he has, for sixty years, claimed to have only been an assistant in an anti-aircraft division. Since the revelation, Grass, a strong critic of Nazi Germany, and an author whose work has urged the country to come to terms with its past, has had his authenticity questioned. People ask, why did he not reveal the information earlier? Why has he kept quiet here, while, when other people did not speak of their past, he was most critical. For many, the deliberate lie of Günter Grass has reduced the credibility of his ideals and his work.

Thirty, A Dialogue –

I think part of me is broken.

                                  Part of you looks broken.

Definitely that part is broken.

Hmm.

Move your arm.

...

Thanks.

This is nice.

This?

Yeah.

Just lying here.

This is nice.

Don't go sleepy.

Sorry.

I wish I had a cigarette.

A smoke would be nice, yeah.

There's not one round, is there?

No. We've given up.

I know.

You ever dream of animals smoking?

No.

Last night, I dreamt of a whole room of them, smoking. Sitting in chairs, at tables, smoking. All the pigs from *Animal Farm*. I swear, I woke up with the taste of cigarette and pig in my mouth.

Pig is gross.

...

...

...

What's the time?

Just after eleven.

Another hour and you'll be thirty.

Trust – When an author writes about something that is based off real events, be it historical or part of their own, personal history, the reader gives the writer their trust that it will be true. At times, I believe that it is this reason why genre fiction, be it crime fiction, fantasy fiction, or romance fiction, is treated with disdain. There is no truth in genre fiction. It is a product of lies. The gender, race, political and sexual leanings of the author have no immediately perceived baring on it. But should an author begin to write about something that is true, every aspect of their life will be scrutinized to ensure that is, indeed, worth the trust of the reader.

Turner, George – The Australian born author George Turner died in 1997, at the age of eighty-one. Having established himself as a mainstream author by winning the prestigious Miles Franklin Award, he turned his attention to science fiction, and there he spent the final twenty years of his writing life. His finest work, I believe, was the novel *Genetic Soldier*, his last novel to be published while he was alive (*Down There in Darkness* was released in 1999, a novel largely incomplete, and best forgotten). What makes *Genetic Soldier* such an interesting book is that it recreates the arrival of the First Fleet, this time in the form of the returning starship *Search*, which has spent seven centuries searching for alternate worlds. The crew returns to Earth to find it vastly altered, but still believing that they have ownership over it. Difficult to find in his native country, Turner's *Genetic Soldier*, along with the remainder of his work, is now, sadly, no longer in print.

Trust, A Dialogue –

You think I look thirty?

I don't know.

...

What does thirty look like?

Health insurance?

You can't look like health insurance.

One of the students was guessing my age today.

She said twenty-five.

Maybe she's trying to pick you up.

Maybe she wants better marks, is more like it.

You reckon I look thirty?

No.

Maybe.

I mean, you don't have any hair.

I didn't have any hair when I was twenty one.

You can't tell age with people. You can't tell a thing about people my looking at them. It's depressing that people judge each other by how they look.

That's not an answer.

It's not a question I have an answer for.

Why you asking, anyway?

You're always on about how you don't want people to judge you by your appearance. That's why you got so much black, and you hate it when people call you mean looking, so why you suddenly care if you look thirty?

Vanity, I guess.

Don't be vain, baby.

That's easy for you to say.

You're not turning thirty.

Yeah, my foot isn't anywhere near that grave.

Tex, Don and Charlie – Under the name Tex, Don and Charlie, Tex Perkins, Don Walker, and Charlie Owen, have released two country studio albums, *Sad But True,* and *All Is Forgiven,* and one live album, *Monday Morning Come Down....* While my interest in country music is fairly limited, I am drawn to this project because of Tex Perkins, and the way he changes his voice and stage presence from project to project. Perkins was first noticed as the front man for the Beasts of Bourbon, a blues punk band, where he prowled across the stage, spitting out words in an angry growl, singing about bringing drugs back in your ass, and being a drop out. He later fronted the more melodic driven Cruel Sea, where he appeared on stage dressed primarily in black, the classic, cool rock musician who was fronting a band. Towards the end of the Cruel Sea, he began releasing solo albums in a urban blues vein, where he would appear on stage in jeans and a t-shirt, and sit on a stool and sing and play guitar. A truly fascinating performer to watch even when releasing country albums.

Transmutation – Nothing is unaltered. Nothing is pure. Nothing is absolute.

Tiptree Jr., James – James Tiptree Jr., born in 1915, was, in fact, Alice Sheldon. She chose the male pseudonym because she was planning to write in the male dominated field of science fiction, and did not want to be singled out due to her gender. Eventually, she would, but not for the reasons she thought. Until 1976, when she revealed the truth, Sheldon's writing was often referred to as being quite masculine. Robert Silverberg, in the introduction to Tiptree's *Warm Worlds and Otherwise*, wrote that the stories within the collection proved without a doubt that Tiptree could not, possibly, be female. After her revelation, however, and where one might have expected criticism as other author hoaxes have resulted in, the science fiction community reacted without terribly much concern. A year later, Sheldon was award the Nebula, and continued to write under the Tiptree name until her suicide, ten years later. Tragically, she killed her ill husband before taking her own life. There remains, in the speculative fiction community, an award named after her pseudonym for fiction relating to gender portrayals.

Truthiness – What is it that I have the authority to write about?

Truth. A Dialogue –

                                      Nearly midnight.

You sound sad.

                                What are you going to do?

In the morning?

I'll get up.

                                        I'll be gone.

You always are.

U

Understanding –

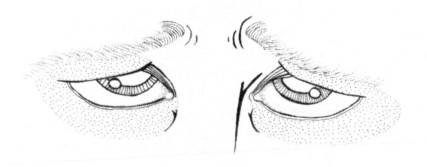

University – I was never meant to go to University, but I didn't want a full time job, either. That opinion was driven home when, with C, we applied for the dole at Blacktown Centrelink. The office is located across from a rundown, faded ice skating rink, and in front of an empty lot filled with shopping trolleys, bottles, and tall grass tangled between them all. In there, we filled in a sheet for unemployment. Our plan was to simply get the money and live off that as we figured out what we wanted to do. Once we filled in the forms, however, we had to do an interview, and I ended up sitting in front of a guy twice my age and grey with responsibility and authority. He was a very serious man, and in his very serious voice, he told me I had no skills, no prospects, and no options. *None*, he repeated. I couldn't get much of a word in, and when I did, he told me that didn't help. It wasn't going well. In fact, it was going horribly. When I left, I had a job interview on Monday, at a hardware store. The whole thing was, frankly, becoming more than a little depressing.

Urinal. Personal Diary Entry, October 12th – *What's the first thing you do when you get out of bed? You take a piss. You wash your hands. You look in the mirror. You try to ignore the bits of your night that cling to you. You hope shaving will cut them away.*

University – I never went to the Hardware Job Interview. Never got unemployment, that time. When I arrived home the phone was ringing, so I picked it up. It took me a while to realise that I was talking to someone from the University of Western Sydney. She was ringing, she said, because I had submitted an essay for scholarship the year before. It was true: Mum had seen it in the paper, and I thought that it would be a chance to get some free money, and wrote an essay. I had not won the scholarship, but instead gotten the runner's up prize, which was a CD voucher. I used it to buy an Alice Cooper album. It was the one and only Alice Cooper album I would ever buy. Months later, and the woman on the phone was telling me that the head of the Humanities department at UWS had taken an interest in me. The Professor had made a place for me, she said. I told her my mark, at least half of what was required to get into the course. The place, I was assured, had been made regardless of my marks. All I had to do was sign up. Two years later, in a course with that Professor, I asked him why he had made the place. Why the effort? I was the only person I knew of that it had happened to, so I was curious. He was a small, wild haired man with thick glasses; but he was shy, and spoke by repeating words and phrases, especially when speaking publicly, which made his lectures painful. 'Oh, yes,' he said, after I asked. We were walking down a narrow path. I was taking a class of his called Chaos Theory and it had just finished. 'There was something in the essay worth the effort. Why did—why did you take the place?' I told him it was because I didn't want to sell hardware.

User. Personal Diary Entry, October 12th – *All the emotions from the night, where did they come from? From the nothing? From a part of me that's not tangible, that cannot be explained with words, and thoughts? No. That's just fucking wank. They come because I want them. They make me feel good. They give me a place. It's an old place, but it's the only place I got right now.*

Umbilical Cords in Your Mind – You believe a vivid memory. It is important to you, so it can't be wrong. A memory of such startling clarity is often referred to as a flashbulb memory, so called because it is like a bulb exploding in your mind, and leaving its imprint on you. However, it has been argued, in the last ten years or so, that the vividness of it is not due to the original moment, but rather to its reinforcement. Knowing where you were when the planes hit the World Trade Centre is further crystallised in your mind because it is repeated, again and again, around you. The same goes for personal memories, though those, it can be said, are nourished by yourself. You replay them. You repeat them. You alter them, slightly, each time, until the imperfections are rubbed away, and you believe only in what is left.

Unrequited – I met G on my third degree, a doctorate. The actual paper and letters of degrees do not matter to me much, but as a way to keep writing, they were good enough. In a country that imports its popular arts, you have got to find different ways to give yourself time, and to explore what you want to do. This was mine. I was at the University of New South Wales this time, which is located next to a racing course, and across from a college for actors. I met G at a community radio station, when she was doing an Arts degree, and I did an interview for her about being a writer in the University system. I sent her an email after. We saw a movie. I think I liked her more than she liked me, at first, but that is how it is sometimes.

Uncertainty – If you watch someone, and they know that they are being watched, they will act a certain way. They will perform, in fact. As if given a narrative that they must act out, they will alter their behaviour to equal a certain set of objectives that they think are appropriate for the moment. Watch a soldier, and he or she will be neat, polite, and obedient. A teenager will profess to like a subject, an event, and claim to not have heard of many things that they have. A parent will be caring and attentive and selfless. From the point of view of the observer, the hope is that if you watch someone long enough, the individual will return to their natural state. Shoes get scuffed. Pornography is found in the history of the computer. Needs go unattended. If you watch long enough, imperfections are revealed. But if you leave early, you'll never see their resolution.

Understanding –

Utopia. Personal Diary Entry, October 12th – *If I don't get up, nothing changes.*

V

Vonnegut, Kurt – Born in 1922, the American satirist, Kurt Vonnegut is responsible for creating the reoccurring character of Kilgore Trout, a science fiction author whose work is largely unread, and found in the pages of pornographic magazines (which possibly paid more than science fiction magazines). Trout, while inspired by science fiction author Theodore Sturgeon, is largely viewed as a fictional version of Vonnegut and the author has described Trout as being someone he once was, and an alter ego; Vonnegut himself began writing science fiction novels and short stories before moving out of the genre. In 1974, well after Vonnegut's exodus from science fiction, *Venus on the Half-Shell*, a novel written by Kilgore Trout, was published. While many assumed that the book was written by Vonnegut himself, the author was instead Philip Jose Farmer, who appeared on the back of the book wearing a fake beard and confederate hat. Vonnegut is reported to have been unhappy with the Trout book once it was published, claiming later that it harmed his literary reputation, though he by all accounts gave his permission to Farmer before the book was written, and the identity of the true author of Kilgore Trout was not kept a secret. But it is unwise to let an alter-ego fall into the hands of anyone but the ego.

Voice – It was written, once, that I have a quiet voice that means business.

Violent. Personal Diary Entry, October 12th – *When the memories aren't there, there's just anger. I can feel it. It sits in my stomach all heavy and hard. There's none of that energy you get some times with hate. It's just heavy. My bed sags more on those mornings. I'm wearing the mattress thin with hate. My jaw hurts on this mornings. I grind my teeth. I can taste the breaking bone. I hate myself. I hate her too. Just a little. Just some. For the absence, you understand.*

Videos – The first night G comes over for dinner, we pull out an old box of videos. VHS. They have cartoons, TV shows, documentaries, and films on them. We are looking for the title of a film that neither of us can remember (later I remember it is *Fallen Angels*) and we try to use the tapes to jog our memories. There, she finds my collection of the original Star Wars trilogy, which she hates with a passion, though I do not know this at the time. Instead, I tell her how my copy of *the Empire Strikes Back* is an illegal dub. It was made in the 80s by my father and his friend, who, one weekend, set up two video recorders and, with a rented a copy of the film, made me one because I loved the first film so much. After I tell her this, G asks me if the copy is still good. Later, we watch some of the film.

Vindictive. Personal Diary Entry, October 12th – *I wrote angry letters. Angry emails. Composed mentally every pissed off thing I would say on the phone. I would have my fucking say. I would fucking tell her what I fucking thought. I would make her fucking understand! I would! I so would! At least, that is what I thought. I thought a lot. I composed in my head. I shook reality. I made everything perfect. Everything came back to the quiet, calm days I woke up in bed, with her smell, with her touch, and now, with her. But they were nothing. Dreams. Memories. Ways to haunt myself. The letters were angry, unfinished scrawls. The emails deleted. The phone calls never made. I told myself everything I felt was normal.*

Vegetarian – G and I became vegetarians, for a year. That was the bet. The challenge. I had made a similar bet with C the previous year, in which we both agreed not eat junk food. Not one bit. Not at all. For a year, we walked into rundown cafes, into sushi bars, into anything that looked different. G loved the idea, wanted to do it herself. So for a year we would be vegetarians and eat every kind of food that wasn't from an animal. For a while it was good, but when the sausages that tasted like sausages but weren't really sausages were introduced, it got ridiculous. They irritated me. So did the bacon that wasn't bacon but tasted like bacon. It was a joke, right? The reason not to eat meat from a living creature was because killing a living creature for food was morally wrong, or at least that is how I took it; but how did that make eating simulated meat any better? How could you be morally superior while eating fake meat? I mean, obviously, if you're eating fake meat, you want to eat real meat, and you like the taste of real meat. In protest of the fake meat, I ate real chicken, and lost the bet. For the rest of the year, I drove us everywhere. I felt I had the moral victory, however.

Validation. Personal Diary Entry, October 12th – *I have done nothing wrong. I keep telling myself that.*

Violence – I have hurt myself, and I will, again. Physical pain blocks emotional pain. When the drugs don't work, there is always a second choice. What has struck me about violence, is how easy it is to access, in all its forms. How more readily available it is to anything else. How much more people are willing to understand it. Outside myself, I have only hurt one person, but when I am angry, when I'm looking for something destructive, it is so easy to find something for the self. Razor blades. Video games. Movies. Target ranges. Martial arts classes. Boxing. Reality TV. I have never had trouble with violence. I have never had trouble making anyone understand it, even when it is nothing but a self destructive tendency. Even then, I am understood.

Vulnerable. A Personal Diary Entry, October 12ᵗʰ – *I HAVE done nothing wrong.*

Vehicle – I have owned two cars in my life. The first was a white Mazda, made in 1974, two years before I was born. I paid fifteen hundred dollars for it and later sold it for three hundred to a pair of guys who were going to do it up after it became so infested with rust that it wouldn't pass registration. My second car was a red Ford Festiva, which I paid eight grand for. I left it in Brisbane.

W

Words – Words lie.

Writer – My year nine English teacher is the first person to read a story of mine and she accuses me of plagiarism. She holds me back after class one day and tells me this, and though I may deny it, she *knows the truth*, because the work is simply too good to be mine. I tell her she is wrong. It is mine. She puts me on detention. After, I get a second lecture on plagiarism, and deny it still. The next day, I am sent to the Head of the English department who, in her smoker's crackling voice, tells me what kind of sin plagiarism is in the world of literature. I tell her I wrote it. She tells me that if I did, then I should be in a higher class. That my marks would be better. 'I don't believe you,' she says, frankly. She threatens me with detention, again, but I refuse to back down. In later years, I read books about English teachers who support their students. How nice these fictions are. In the office, the Head of the English department ashes her cigarette, then, quietly, threatens to call my mother. I give her the number. Two weeks later, and another two meetings, I am given my assignment back with the grudging acceptance that I did write it. On the top is the mark, 49 out of 50. It is the only time I have ever thought I deserved a higher mark. For the hassle, you understand.

Words – There is no truth in words. Meaning changes due to culture, time, and tone: a word is an empty shell until it is filled by the individual. Then, once fired by the originator, the word turns blank yet again, and fills with meaning only when it hits the receiver.

Language is a parasite. It buries under our skin. Leaves traps. Sinks into your subconscious. Depending on the strength of the parasite, it draws out the old meanings, leaves the new. Because of this, language is constantly changing. It is slippery. Untrustworthy. It is the first thing I learnt as a writer.

Writer – My early fiction is bad. Though I sold my first story when I was eighteen, and by the time I was twenty four, had sold a chapbook, around fifteen short stories, a few bits of poetry, some reviews, and two columns (one on a website, one in a newspaper) the work was undisciplined, unfocused, and stylistically excessive. It had begun, in many ways, to feel like a job. A poorly paid, under appreciated, shitty job. After my chemical rebirth, I wondered why I was doing it. Why I was putting in so much time. Why it mattered. Then came R, and the word *child*, with its meanings, and its responsibility. The responsibility I had avoided. In my mind, the unreal child lingered, attached to imaginary umbilical cords, growing, fattening, demanding. It demanded not that it be acknowledged, or that it be treated, but that its existence have a purpose. It could not sit in the back of my head slowly turning rotten. The word could not be allowed to decay. The word child had begun to convey a meaning of choice, of showing how, at one moment, life could have gone one way, but because of choice, had instead gone another. Child meant choice. Choice meant responsibility. Responsibility meant writing.

Words – S knows the history of words. One day, as she sits on a tram in Melbourne, all the noise of the city at night filtering through the phone, I tell her how I think words change, how language is personal and filled with meanings, meanings that I plan to drag out, exploit, and use. I tell her how I plan to lay my own personal language out and find its connective tissue. I tell her in a breathless rush. I tell her and then I pause. On the other side of the phone she is silent. Then, finally, she says, 'Are you okay?'

Writer – No more half measures. No more pulling back. No more worrying if I haven't gone far enough, or if I have gone too far. No more worrying about what will happen if I fail. It doesn't matter if I do. No one was watching. No one is ever watching the unknown and unwanted. There is no money involved and that is fine. Anonymity was freedom. Freedom means that there are no constraints. Freedom meant fuck you, fuck me, just plain fuck it. Write, and write with passion, write with everything you have. Don't write as if it were a job. Some days will suck, some days will bite, but I will not phone it in like I have done so many shifts at a job, trading time for cash. If I wanted a job, I could get one. Writing is not a job. I will not treat it like such.

Welles, Orson (Surrogate Father Figure #3) – Born in 1915, dead in 1985, Orson Welles is the model of failure. Having begun his career so brilliantly on the stage and radio, Welles found, in film, a medium that he loved, but which he would fail so brightly at. In an interview at the end of his life, he noted how the majority of his career had been spent hustling backers for money so that he could play with his expensive paint box ten percent of the time. But when he was able to secure funding, he spent the other half of his time fighting, and more often than not losing, the battle for creative control—an offer given to him at the very beginning of his film career with *Citizen Kane*, and repeated only a few times during the rest of his life. The result is that Orson Welles' body of work is fragmented, incomplete, and what is complete, while demonstrating flashes of brilliance, labours under budget and studio constraints. His articulate vision is so often rendered inarticulate that, by the end of his life, Welles, now at times so overweight that he could not walk, was a curiousity, a creator locked in a time and place, and allowed out only to talk about this time period. He would be invited out to dinner by new creators, men and women who idolised portions of his work, but who were only interested in him as an artifact, and who would deny him funding to create again.

Written – I do not make much money out of what I write, but that does not matter to me. I have met those who make money, and they work in a way I do not want to. I write what I write, I write it how I want, when I want, and whatever happens after that, happens.

Wake – When I'm dead, I won't care what you do with my work.

Words – Words hurt.

X

X is Where You Sign Your Name

Form 9

Births, Deaths and Marriages Registration Act 2003 (Section 30)

Queensland Government
Department of Justice and Attorney-General

CAUSE OF DEATH CERTIFICATE
Please print clearly, using BLOCK letters
To the Registrar-General, Brisbane

Office Use Only
TB: ☐
Date Rec:
District Code:
Registration No:

(Note: This certificate shall not be given without authorisation of the Coroner in relation to a reportable death. This certificate must also be completed for a stillborn child (see Note below). If particulars are unknown, write "UNKNOWN". All items marked with an asterisk (*) are for statistical or administrative purposes only and will not appear in the Register of Deaths. Form distribution: Original (white) to the Registrar-General or the person arranging for the disposal of the body; Duplicate (blue) to the person arranging for the disposal of the body; Triplicate (yellow) to be retained by Doctor. Form should be completed within 2 working days of the death.)

I, _____, a registered Doctor:

(a) For a stillborn child*:	or	(b) For any other deceased person (including a neonatal death †)*:
☐ was present at the stillbirth; or		☐ attended the deceased person when alive; or
☐ examined the stillborn child's body.		☑ examined the deceased's body; or
		☐ considered the deceased's medical history and the circumstances of the death.

and certify that: **Geraldine Rachel Lee** (full name of deceased) was aged 1979 / 3 / 1 (Y / M / D)

and born on: ___ / ___ / ___ (if known)* sex: M (F) (circle one) and I believe that he/she died on: 2006 / 3 / 3

at: 9.56 pm For stillborn or neonate: time of birth* _____ time of death* _____

In my opinion, the probable cause of death is as stated below in section 'A' or 'B':

'A' – (for a stillborn child or neonate†):

1(a)	Main disease or condition in foetus or neonate	
1(b)	Other diseases or conditions in foetus or neonate	
1(c)	Main maternal disease or condition affecting foetus or neonate	
1(d)	Other maternal diseases or conditions affecting foetus or neonate	
2	Other relevant circumstances	

Underlying Cause of Death*:

'B' – (for any other deceased person):			**Duration of last illness** (approximate interval between onset and death)
Disease or condition directly leading to death: (This means the final disease or condition which caused death – NOT the mode of dying such as heart failure, respiratory failure, etc, UNLESS explained by Antecedent Causes below.)	1(a)	SEVERE HEAD INJURY	Immediate
		due to, or as a consequence of	
	1(b)	MOTOR VEHICLE ACCIDENT	Immediate
		due to, or as a consequence of	
Antecedent Causes – morbid conditions, if any, giving rise to the above cause, stating the underlying condition last.	1(c)		
		due to, or as a consequence of	
	1(d)		
		due to, or as a consequence of	
	1(e)		
Other Significant Conditions – contributing to the death, but not related to the underlying cause given in Part 1.	2		

Date and type of **operation** in the last 4 weeks* ___ / ___ / ___

Pregnancy: Was the deceased **pregnant** within 6 weeks of death?* ☐ No ☑ Yes

Was the deceased **pregnant** between 6 weeks and 12 months of death?* ☐ No ☐ Yes

Does the body of the deceased pose a **cremation risk** under the Cremations Act 2003*? ☐ No ☐ Yes _____ (please specify eg. pacemaker)

Is the death a **reportable death** under the Coroners Act 2003 (CA)*?
☐ No
☐ No, Coroner has advised death not reportable under s.26(5)(a) of CA.
☑ Yes, issue of this certificate was authorised under s.12(2)(b) of the CA.

Note: Please complete a Perinatal Supplement (to Cause of Death Certificate) (Form 9A) if the above information relates to a child who was stillborn (of at least 20 weeks gestation or 400 grams weight at birth) or who died within 28 days after birth (neonate) †

_____ 3 / 3 / 06
(Insert name of Coroner who advised or who authorised this Certificate and Date)

Non-Coronial Autopsy Consented by Next of Kin*
☐ Carried out ☐ To be carried out ☑ Not to be carried out

Was the deceased of Aboriginal or Torres Strait Islander origin?
(If of both Aboriginal and Torres Strait Islander origin, tick both 'Yes' boxes)*
☑ No ☐ Yes, Aboriginal origin ☐ Yes, Torres Strait Islander origin

Doctor's Signature _____
Date 4 / 3 / 06
Initials and Surname _____
Professional Qualification(s)* _____
Address _____
Telephone _____

Form 9 Ver. 1 01/02/2004

Note: This Certificate must be issued without charge

Y

Yeah. Personal Diary Entry, 12th October – *I lie in bed like this. I sleep beside the memories. My fingers touch the phantom of her. I haunt myself because it makes things easier. I like the lies.*

Yourself –

Yesterday. Personal Diary Entry, 12ᵗʰ October – *Everything is beginning to fade. I ask myself, is that how she smelt? Did she really taste that way? Was her laugh just like that? I try to hold on to as much as I can but there are new things every day, new bits of life filtering through my consciousness. I got into a car the other day with D and I didn't tense up. I didn't react. I just sat. I talked. It was as if nothing had happened.*

Year – There are three hundred and sixty five days in a year. Eight thousand, seven hundred and sixty hours. Five hundred and twenty five thousand and six hundred minutes. Thirty one million, five hundred and thirty six thousand seconds. There is a lot of time in which you can hide from yourself.

You. Personal Diary Entry, 12ᵗʰ October – *I drove the car. I was always driving the car in Brisbane. On the night she died, it was still the case. We had just left Earth, angry at each other. Angry and pissed off. It was one of those warm empty nights in Brisbane, a nice night, but neither of us was saying anything. We were just angry. In the car, G began going through the CDs in short, sharp movements. I drove. I was speeding, which I knew she hated, but she refused to say anything. Every now and then I would glance over and see her lips tightly pressed, her fingers down over the plastic of an album, a mix of anger and fear. The last time I looked down and then up, a semi trailer had come down off a ramp. It was a dark block suddenly cutting across the road, running right in front of us like a wall. We had the red light. I don't know how I missed it. I slammed on the brakes, but it was too late, much too late, and so I turned the wheel and I did (I so fucking did) I turned it so my side of the car didn't impact. I made that decision. I made that choice. and a moment before hitting the long, thick trailer with its thick edges, I remember clearly thinking, FUCK YOU.*

Yeah, Yeah, Yeahs, The – In the car. After. After the crash. In the silence. In the glass. In the blood. An album. G had been holding it. The Yeah, Yeah, Yeahs. A yellow and purple and red cover. *Show Your Bones.*

Yearn. Personal Diary Entry, October 12th – *Nothing you do or say takes back a moment.*

Yasusada Araki – Araki Yasusada was a Japanese poet who survived the atomic bomb that America dropped on Hiroshima. Having died in the 1972, his poetry was discovered by a son who had the work translated, and published in American literary journals. Yasusada was, of course, a fake poet, the invention of an American academic. The controversy that arises, however, is that critics have argued that Yasusada's poetry was only published because of political correctness. American literary journals, unable to escape the latent cultural guilt of being part of the nation that was responsible for the horrors of Hiroshima, responded by publishing the work of a "survivor". It was as if they sought to make amends by giving him a public voice.

Yield – If you accept that truth is subjective, unreliable, and inconsistent, then do we still have a responsibility to it?

Yes? – No?

Z

Zero, Year – Year Zero refers to the institution of a new political regime in a country. It is not a natural beginning, however, as a Year Zero is created through the removal of the already existing government. The Year Zero is, then, the first steps of a new world after violence, whether those who have been raised in the area wish it or not.

Zoetrope –

Zone – I have not been to my father's grave in ten years, but L drives me out there on a cold day in July. I have asked. In silence, we drift up the narrow road, neatly mowed lawns stretching around us. At the top, she stops, and we get out. After a while, she asks me if I am okay, and I tell her I am trying to remember where the grave is. I think it is next to a tree, but there are a lot of trees, and so, for the next twenty minutes, we walk past each tree in the area I think the plaque is in. It becomes clear that I have forgotten. Shaking my head, I tell L it doesn't matter, that we should go. I feel foolish. She tells me no, we'll continue looking. We pass dirty, forgotten plaques with pictures on them. We pass clean plaques with flowers. We pass plaques with toys next to them. Eventually, we find my father's. It is dirty. I clean it. I stare at it. After a while, I realise I have nothing to say, and I wonder why I came here, before I realise that it was guilt. I have come because of guilt. I have spent too much time at another grave.

Zero – *Terra nullius* is the idea that a piece of land is empty before it is colonised. It argues that because no one has lived on it, it is therefore without sovereignty. In reality, *terra nullius* argues that no civilized group of people were living on the land, with the term civilized being applied to anyone who didn't have a society similar to that of the invading culture. Australia used *terra nullius* to justify ignoring Aboriginal ownership of the country in the years after invasion. This meant teaching history as if Aboriginal culture did not exist. Australia is, for example, still discovered by Captain Cook, as if it had somehow not existed before, and that an entire culture and history had not been living on the land for thousands of years. *Terra nullius* is not so much an idea, but the myth of unoccupied land, and of a time when there was nothing before current events.

Zither – G collected instruments. She played for fun, lacking the dedication and, yes, the skill to take it as anything more. After her funeral, and while I am preparing to move, I am not sure what to do with the collection, but eventually, I give some to her mother, and to her friends. I keep the zither. It is made in India, and the wood is a deep, deep red; at times, I think it is warm to the touch. I pluck the strings, but I do not know if they are in tune properly.

Zoetrope –

Zenith – In the months approaching his thirtieth birthday, Sydney based author Ben Peek wrote an autobiography, *Twenty-Six Lies/One Truth*. Splitting the slim book into three different threads, Peek detailed his life growing up Sydney, the night that his partner, Geraldine Lee, died in a road accident, and series of vignettes about authors who had lied about their own origins and their work. The title of the book played upon the falsehoods of the authors that were detailed in each chapter, and also hinted at Peek's own life detailed within. Yet, while portions of the book were publicly verifiable by Peek's own interviews and those with his friends (though Peek himself refused to discuss the validity of book itself after its publication), many critics were quick to point that the one obvious falsehood in the author's life was that he had never lived in Brisbane.

Zero – Return to nothing. Leave the past behind. Forget everything that you were. Ask yourself, if you woke with amnesia, would you like the person you were told about? And if not, what would you do? Would you recreate yourself?

Zoetrope –

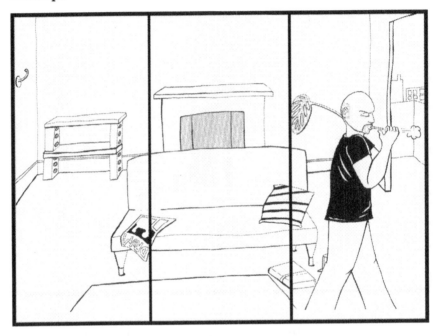

Zimbabwe – In July 2006, Zimbabwe continued to leave behind its colonist, Western values, and lifted the ban on witchcraft.

Most of My Friends Are White:
A Character Description Key

Because of the nature that *Twenty-Six Lies/One Truth* is written, detailed descriptions of the people involved in the author's life were difficult to include without making the prose ugly. To rectify this, the following is a list of character descriptions, including a short biographical note. Blacked out entries indicate that the individual is no longer active in the author's life, for better or worse, and the reader should use their own imagination.

A – The daughter of Australian born hippies. Small, busty, reddish brown hair, white. Dylan Thomas, she says, did not die early enough.

B – A big, bald man, with an auburn haired goatee. White. The author.

C – Tall, lanky, brown haired man. The son of a Dutch and Maltese parents, his skin colour is a dark, Mediterranean white. In his house are old, polished football trophies. Around the rooms are footballs, full sized, half sized, and made from beans. He lets you throw them in the house if you are over the age of eighteen. Currently called as a witness in a murder trial.

D – Born to Australian and English parents in Australia. Standing at six foot four, he is a lean, long faced figure with brownish blond hair. One son. Both son and father are white. Recently learnt the monetary gains involved in being a self employed pornographer were quite high. In addition, would only have to work two days a week.

E – ███████████████████████████████████

F – Born to Australian parents, but dead in 1986. Cancer. A big, bald, sun browned, white man who had, once, been brown haired. The author's father.

G – Small, petite girl, with mouse brown hair died blonde. Mother Australian, Father white New Zealander. White. Tattoos of red and black stars splattered around her left wrist. Said that her parents resented her birth, which is why they gave her the name that they did. Denied by mother strongly.

H – ████████████████████████████████████
███

I – Used by author to reference self throughout book. See 'B' for more details.

J – Slim, dark haired male, the son of Australian and Maltese parents. Describes his own skin colour as woggish. Well dressed, intelligent, articulate, but with a dislike for live music. Once made mescaline in kitchen. Willing to do it again. Lives with X. Maintains that he is not obsessed with Jesus.

K – Blonde haired dyed red, dyed black, dyed brown, dyed blonde. New each month. Of medium build. White skinned. Currently working on a resort in Florida. The author's sister.

L – Brown haired, medium build, white, the daughter of Irish and British parents. Likes her men to be living in Mountains and rugged. Will deny if asked.

M – Small, grey haired, born in Britain. White. Bright blue eyes. The author's mother. Currently on her eighth rescue dog. Strange, dark vans with veterinarians lurk in the street outside her house.

N – ███████████████████████████████████
████████████████

O – Small, blonde haired, white, the daughter of Australian parents. Soft, musical voice. Black Sabbath fan. Lives with U. Age, she complains, is killing her ability to drink.

P – ████████████████████████████████████

Q – Petite, dark haired, born in Vietnam to Vietnamese parents. Asian. Loves live music. One tattoo on back. Slowly rebuilding her photography equipment after it was stolen when her apartment was broken into.

R – ██████████████████████████████

S – Dark haired, curved, white, the daughter of Italian and Australian parents. Likes cute shoes. A writer. Infamously compared living in Sydney to dating an expensive, disease ridden hooker. Does *not* live in Sydney.

T – Australian born, Vietnamese parents, Asian. Medium build. Dislikes American comics. American comics are not for girls, she says. Obsession with Harry Potter slash fiction slightly unacceptable. Saved by still fine music tastes.

U – Born in an Australian town to an Australian born Reverend and his Australian born wife. White, brown haired, big man with big, flat feet. Feet for walking on hot sand, pavement, and without shoes. Lives with O. In a suit cuts a series of straight, fine lines.

V – American born, dark skinned, but white, with reddish-brown haired. Adopted. Member of Mensa.

W – ███████████████████████████████
████████████████

X – Tall, dark haired, the child of white Australians. Lives with J. Is currently studying for a pilot license and no longer pretends to be a woman for men online.

Y – White, blonde, medium build American, the daughter of white Americans. Maintains that *Middlemarch* is one of the finest novels written. Hates being photographed. No longer writes erotica.

Z – Petite, dark haired, born in China. Chinese born parents. Artist with artist's long, fine fingers. Changes eye colour with contacts. Blue, green, grey. Nothing, she says, need be defined by what it looks like.

Acknowledgements

This book could not have been completed without the help of C.L. Likewise, I am ever thankful for S.C. for her tagline. K.W. was the link to A.B. and is thus responsible for so much good karma it cannot be explained here. A.M. gave the fantastic, cool as all get out cover, and cannot be thanked enough. A.B. bought her special magic and special skills and the book would be a pale thing without it. Lastly, a final thanks goes to D.L., who had faith in the project and backed it, and who didn't once object to the long and seemingly random emails about it that were sent at two in the morning.

About the Author

Ben Peek is the author of the dystopian novel, *Black Sheep*. His short fiction has appeared in the anthologies *Polyphony Six*, *Leviathan Four: Cities*, *Agog! Ripping Reads*, and the magazines *Aurealis*, *Full Unit Hookup*, and *Fantasy Magazine*. In addition to that, his work has been reprinted in the Year's Best Australian Science Fiction and Fantasy. He keeps a blog at *http://benpeek.livejournal.com*.

About the Artists

Since the beginning of 2005, Andrew Macrae, another Australian writer, has been doing all his writing on a typewriter. This all started with a dream about a typewriter he had as a child, a machine he loved. It had belonged to his grandmother. When she went blind after a stroke, they decided they'd try to teach her to type. Well, that didn't really work out so the machine ended up at his parents' place and he used to love playing on it.

In the dream, that machine was full of joy and magic. He leant over and took a big sniff of it and the smell of ink and solvents and machine oil nearly knocked him out. So Andy decided this dream was telling him something and he started collecting typewriters, and soon producing art.

The cover for this book was done on the very same typewriter he played with as a child.

⊕

Anna Brown is an artist and illustrator who lives with her family in Port Kembla, New South Wales.

OTHER TITLES AVAILABLE FROM WHEATLAND PRESS

ANTHOLOGIES

POLYPHONY 1, Edited by Deborah Layne and Jay Lake. Volume one in the critically acclaimed slipstream/cross-genre series will feature stories from Maureen McHugh, Andy Duncan, Carol Emshwiller, Lucius Shepard and others.

POLYPHONY 2, Edited by Deborah Layne and Jay Lake. Volume two in the critically acclaimed slipstream/cross-genre series will feature stories from Alex Irvine, Theodora Goss, Jack Dann, Michael Bishop and others.

POLYPHONY 3, Edited by Deborah Layne and Jay Lake. Volume three in the critically acclaimed slipstream/cross-genre series will feature stories from Jeff Ford, Bruce Holland Rogers, Ray Vukcevich, Robert Freeman Wexler and others.

POLYPHONY 4, Edited by Deborah Layne and Jay Lake. Fourth volume in the critically acclaimed slipstream/cross-genre series with stories from Alex Irvine, Lucius Shepard, Michael Bishop, Forrest Aguirre, Theodora Goss, Stepan Chapman and others.

POLYPHONY 5, Edited by Deborah Layne and Jay Lake. The world Fantasy Award-nominated fifth volume in the critically acclaimed slipstream/cross-genre series with stories from Jeff VanderMeer, Ray Vukcevich, Bruce Holland Rogers, Leslie What and more.

THE NINE MUSES, Edited by Forrest Aguirre and Deborah Layne. Original anthology featuring some of the top women writers in science fiction, fantasy and experimental fiction, including Kit Reed, Ursula Pflug, Jai Clare, Jessica Treat, and Ruth Nestvold. With an introductory essay by Elizabeth Hand.

TEL: STORIES, Jay Lake Ed. An anthology of experimental fiction with authors to be announced.

ALL STAR ZEPPELIN ADVENTURE STORIES, David Moles and Jay Lake Eds. Original zeppelin stories by Jim Van Pelt, Leslie What, and others; one reprint, "You Could Go Home Again" by Howard Waldrop.

Single-Author Collections

The Keyhole Opera, Bruce Holland Rogers. A collection of short-short stories by the master of the form. Includes the World Fantasy Award-winning story "Don Ysidro" from *Polyphony 4*.

The Beasts of Love: Stories by Steven Utley With an introduction by Lisa Tuttle. Utley's love stories spanning the past twenty years; a brilliant mixture of science fiction, fantasy and horror.

Dream Factories and Radio Pictures, Howard Waldrop. Waldrop's stories about early film and television reprinted in one volume.

Greetings From Lake Wu, Jay Lake and Frank Wu. Collection of stories by Jay Lake with original illustrations by Frank Wu.

Twenty Questions, Jerry Oltion. Twenty brilliant works by the Nebula Award-winning author of "Abandon in Place."

American Sorrows, Jay Lake. Four longer works by the Hugo and Campbell nominated author; includes his Hugo nominated novelette, "Into the Gardens of Sweet Night."

Twenty Six Lies/One Truth, Ben Peek. A distorted experimental autobiography.

Nonfiction

Weapons of Mass Seduction, Lucius Shepard. A collection of Shepard's film reviews. Some have previously appeared in print in the *Magazine of Fantasy and Science Fiction*; most have only appeared online at *Electric Story*.

Novel

Paradise Passed, Jerry Oltion. The crew of a colony ship must choose between a ready-made paradise and one they create for themselves. A finalist for the 2005 Endeavor Award.

For Ordering Information Visit:
WWW.WHEATLANDPRESS.COM

CPSIA information can be obtained at www.ICGtesting.com
Printed in the USA
LVOW021631090613

337689LV00013B/597/A

9 780975 590386